'This sublime, shimmering Blakeian fantasy — for children and adults alike — thrills, enlarges and heals the soul in equal measure. **An out-and-out masterpiece'**
Piers Torday

'Tyger is **next level excellent** — and Dave McKean's illustrations dovetail perfectly and beautifully with the story. **This book is a gem'**
Malorie Blackman

'You wait years and years for a **masterpiece** and then one comes along'
Frank Cottrell-Boyce

'A profound, Blake-inspired novel, that's also a simple thrilling tale of a boy and a girl and a Tyger. **A triumph!'**
Jacqueline Wilson

'Breathtaking, in turns heartbreaking and achingly beautiful. Imagination-stirring, wise and thought-provoking ... **Perfection'**
Sophie Anderson

'I LOVED it so much. **A masterpiece** of a story: beautiful, brilliant, perfect!'
Peter Bunzl

'Readers will fall in love with Tyger and through her their hearts will be strengthened and hope-light recharged ... **a timeless classic'**
Sita Brahmachari

TYGER

by SF Said

www.davidficklingbooks.com

Also by SF Said

Varjak Paw
The Outlaw Varjak Paw
Phoenix

TYGER
is a
DAVID FICKLING BOOK

First published in Great Britain in 2022 by
David Fickling Books,
31 Beaumont Street,
Oxford, OX1 2NP

Text © SF Said, 2022
Illustrations © Dave McKean, 2022

978-1-78845-283-0
1 3 5 7 9 10 8 6 4 2

Papers used by David Fickling Books are from
well-managed forests and other responsible sources.

DAVID FICKLING BOOKS Reg. No. 8340307

A CIP catalogue record for this book is
available from the British Library.
Printed and bound in Great Britain by Clays, Ltd, Elcograf S.p.A

TYGER

SF Said

Illustrated by Dave McKean

David Fickling Books

31 Beaumont Street
Oxford OX1 2NP, UK

It happened in the 21st Century,

when London was still the capital of an Empire,

and the Empire still ruled the world . . .

Chapter One

It was the week before Midwinter. The rain was lashing down, and the narrow streets of Soho were deep with puddles. Although it was midday, the sky over London was iron grey. Clouds of smoke hung heavy up above, as always.

Adam Alhambra wasn't looking at that bleak Midwinter sky. He was looking at the checkpoint up ahead of him, and shivering. He huddled into his coat, but the wind cut through it like a whip. And that wasn't the only thing that made him feel cold.

He could see the soldier there, behind the metal bars and railings. He could hear his stern voice, turning people back from the boundary that separated Soho from the rest of London. As Adam watched, biting down on his pencil, a whole family was being marched away at gunpoint, not allowed to leave the Ghetto.

'Next!'

And now it was his turn. Adam put his pencil behind his ear, and stepped up for inspection, under a row of Union Jacks and a portrait of the Emperor.

The soldier was a guardsman in a red coat, with a bristling white moustache. He looked Adam up and down, taking in his skin, his hair, his eyes. The fact that everything about him was just a little different, just a little darker. Then he looked at Adam's papers, saw his name, and here it came . . .

'*Alhambra?*' said the soldier. 'And where are you from, boy?'

'Um – London, sir,' said Adam, trying to sound calm, and failing.

'You know what I mean,' said the soldier. 'Where are you really from?'

Adam looked down. 'My parents came here from the Middle East, sir,' he said, 'but I've lived in London all my life.'

'The Middle East.' The soldier frowned. 'Isn't that where camels used to come from?'

'Camels?' said Adam, mystified. 'I don't know, sir. I don't know anything about the Middle East.

I'm just doing the deliveries for my family's shop, Alhambra & Company. They're depending on me to do them.' He held up his bag, to show the soldier the parcels that were packed so carefully inside.

'Where are the shop's papers?' said the soldier.

'Oh – right here, sir!' Adam fumbled in his pocket for the documents. But as he pulled them out, a little scrap of paper fell out with them, and fluttered to the floor.

Adam's heart thumped. Quick as he could, he scooped it up, and shoved it back into his pocket.

'Was that a drawing?' said the soldier. 'What do you think you are – an artist?'

Adam's cheeks burned. His mouth went dry. 'No, no, sir, of course not,' he said. 'Please. Here are the shop's papers, see?'

The soldier gave him a long, hard look. He looked at the documents even longer and harder. But finally he grunted, and waved Adam through. 'Go on then, camel boy,' he said. 'Don't start any trouble.'

'Thank you, sir,' Adam made himself say, as he went through the checkpoint, and came out onto Oxford Street.

And here, on the other side of the checkpoint, everything was different. People were shopping on the wide open street. Adults were going to work.

Children were going to school. No one was stopping them, searching them, asking them questions.

For a moment, he wished he could be one of them. Just an ordinary British boy, on his way to school. Someone who could go anywhere he wanted, and do anything he dreamed.

But he was a foreigner, and he had a job to do.

He began to run. He raced up Oxford Street, past the grand department stores, onto Tottenham Court Road. Some of the people he passed gave him the same look as the soldier. He could feel their eyes on his skin. *Keep your head down*, his father always said. *Eye contact only makes it worse. Don't look at anyone, or anything, or—*

CRASH!

'Look where you're going!'

Oh no. Adam looked up to see a lean, hungry-looking man, staring down at him with cold blue eyes.

'Sorry, sir,' said Adam – but the man grinned. His white teeth gleamed.

'Relax!' he said brightly. 'Here, I want to show you something.' He put an arm round Adam's shoulder and steered him off the main road, into a side street.

Adam went with him, grateful that he wasn't in trouble. But doubts were gnawing at his mind. The streets around Tottenham Court Road were grimier and less grand than Oxford Street. There was nothing to see; just thick brick walls, blackened by chimney smoke. No one else was walking here. Something wasn't right.

'Now then,' said the man, as thunder rumbled in the sky. 'Give me your bag, and all your money, and I might just let you live.'

Adam gasped. The man's grip on his shoulder was very tight now, and he was blocking the way back to the road.

'Help!' Adam shouted. But no one on the main road even turned to look.

'Who do you think would help a foreigner?' The man's grin grew wider. 'Now give me that bag, you cockroach.'

Adam's heart hammered.

Desperately, he twisted.

Turned.

And tore himself free.

He ran in the only direction he could: down the side street. But it was a dead end, and it ended at the gates of the dump. A big block of common land, filled with stinking rubbish.

Behind him, he could hear the man's footsteps, pounding on the pavement, hunting him down through the rain.

So he ran through the iron gates of the dump, through heaps of bin bags and crushed tin cans, shattered glass and torn-up posters. The man kept coming, closer and closer, chasing him deeper into the dump.

Lightning slashed the sky. In its glare, Adam saw a little wooden doorway, hidden behind a mountain of ashes.

He plunged through it into darkness.

Broken windows flashed past him as he ran through the rooms of an empty, ruined building. Then a wall loomed up before him. There were no doors except the one he'd come in by. There was no way out. He was trapped in here, and all alone.

He turned to see the man stalking through the door behind him, something glinting in his hand. A knife.

A metallic taste filled Adam's mouth. '*HELP!*' he screamed –

– and then something roared above his head, louder than the thunder.

Chapter Two

It was very dark in the ruined building. But as Adam looked up, his whole body shaking, he saw two points of light above him.

The lights blinked, like eyes.

And then something erupted out of the darkness, moving so fast, he saw only a blur at first. A streak of black and gold, leaping down from the roof beams to land on all four paws beside him.

An animal! A gigantic animal stood by his side, growling at the man with the knife. With one huge stride, she put herself between him and Adam. Then she threw back her head and roared, as if protecting Adam from the knife.

The man screamed. He ran. He fled through the

door he'd come in by, and was gone.

Adam couldn't run. The animal still stood between him and the door. He could only stand there, staring at her, his senses filling with a sweet, high, musky scent, like honeysuckle growing wild. In her presence, everything else just melted away, even his fear.

His skin was prickling and his eyes were wide. But inside him was a feeling stranger than fear. For this animal had come down from the darkness to defend him. Why?

And . . . what *was* she?

A flash of lightning revealed more of her form. She was ten feet long from her whiskers to her tail. So broad, she filled the doorway. Her fur was fiery gold with coal-black stripes.

Time seemed to stop as she turned to look at Adam, and Adam looked back at her. He couldn't look away. He'd never been so close to any animal before, let alone one so huge and wild.

Her eyes burned like liquid golden fire. They were shining with a light that was different to any light he'd ever seen. Yet he thought he saw pain inside them, too. And now that she was facing him, he could see that she was wounded. There was blood on her fur, between her stripes, dripping wet and red.

He breathed in sharply. Whatever she was – this animal was wounded.

She shuddered as a blast of thunder shook the building. She turned and snapped at something over her shoulder, then growled when she couldn't reach it. As she twisted and turned, Adam crept round to one side –

– and froze as he saw the shaft of an arrow, sticking out of her shoulder. On the other side, he could see the arrowhead.

This animal had been hunted. Someone had shot her, trying to kill her. The point of the arrow had passed right through her. All around it, the blood was dripping.

Adam's throat went tight. She would die if that arrow stayed inside her. And she couldn't get it out herself. She had saved his life – but she needed help, even more than he did.

Lightning flashed again. Thunder broke above the ruined building. The animal turned to face Adam. She stood very, very still, and looked him straight in the eye.

Every hair on his head prickled. But she didn't move a muscle. Didn't even twitch her tail. She just kept looking at him, impossibly sharp focus in those golden eyes.

Slowly, as if in a dream, he held out a hand towards her.

Still she didn't move.

He reached closer. And closer. He could see now that the arrowhead was broad and barbed. It would never go back through. He had to pull it out instead.

Adam's mouth was dry as dust as he touched the arrow's shaft. The animal held herself absolutely still as he snapped off the shaft, below the wound, and began to pull very carefully at the arrowhead, drawing it inch by inch from her flesh and fur –

– and still there was more, but he just kept pulling, and pulling – until finally, it came all the way out.

The animal sighed a huge sigh of relief. She slumped to the ground, and began to lick her shoulder, licking and licking with her tongue, trying to stop the bleeding as the rain streamed down outside.

Adam slumped down beside her. His knees felt weak as water. But somehow, he had done it. He had got the arrow out.

'I think you're going to be all right,' he said, to himself as much as to her.

And that was when she spoke, in a voice as clear and close as his own heart, thumping in his throat.

'I thank you,' she said. 'I thank you, O Guardian, for your help.'

Chapter Three

Adam stared at the animal who lay before him in the ruined building. In the whole world now, there was nothing but him and this impossible animal. The animal who had just spoken.

Was he dreaming? He reached out to touch her again. Felt her fur beneath his fingers. Massive muscles underneath. He could feel the beating of her heart. And as that sweet, high, honeysuckle scent filled his mind, he realized the scent was hers. He'd never had a dream so vivid he could smell it, or hold it in his hands.

'What's your name?' he whispered.

'I have been known by many names,' she said. 'But you may call me . . . *Tyger*.'

Adam's scalp tingled as he heard that voice again. It made him feel strange and shy.

'Tyger?' he said. 'But – tygers are extinct. They were all hunted down, a long time ago.'

The tyger stared at him with eyes like golden fire.

'Tell me,' she said, after a while. 'Why are you here?'

'I was hiding from that robber,' said Adam. 'No one else would help me, because I'm a foreigner . . .' He cleared his throat. 'But what about you, Tyger? Why are you here, and not locked up in a cage somewhere? Did you escape?'

The tyger blinked. Her tail thumped behind her. Her whiskers probed the air.

'What sort of world is this?' she said. 'And what sort of Guardian are you?'

'What sort of what?' said Adam, confused.

The tyger turned to gaze up at a window. He followed her gaze. The glass was long gone. Creeping vines had grown all over it, but in the gaps, he could glimpse fragments of the sky.

'I see,' said the tyger at last. 'You are not a Guardian, are you? I felt sure they had arrived.' She glanced back at the crumbling doorway, and the thick white webs that ran across it. 'In all the time I have been hiding here,' she said, 'you are the first to find me. But my enemy's agents are forever on my trail. Please, tell no one I am here.'

Adam felt dizzy. He didn't understand everything the tyger was saying. But he did understand she had risked herself to save his life.

'I won't tell anyone,' he said. 'I promise.'

The tyger settled down on her paws. Her tail curled around her, and she began to lick her wound again in silence. Adam watched, mesmerized by the patterns of her stripes. They were perfectly symmetrical, rippling down both sides of her body like currents flowing down a stream.

His mind was full of questions. But it was clear that the tyger didn't want to talk any more. So he tried to imagine her story for himself: where she'd really come from, who her enemies were, and who these Guardians might be.

His head swam. He felt out of his depth. The only thing he knew for sure was that he wanted her to survive. He wanted to keep her secret, keep her safe, at least until her Guardians arrived.

They sat there quietly together, the two of them, as the rain came down outside the ruin. Gradually, the storm passed. The thunder and lightning moved on, and there was just a steady stream of raindrops on the roof.

The tyger's eyes closed. Her breathing deepened, as if she was falling asleep. Adam stood up slowly – but at once, her ears went sharp, and her eyes flicked open again.

'I must recover my strength,' she said. 'But if you wish . . . you may return here. And perhaps you might help me once more.'

'I will!' said Adam. 'I'll come back as soon as I can, and make sure you're all right. Can I bring you anything? Some food, or water? Or maybe something for that wound?'

The tyger shook her head, and yawned a massive yawn. 'Just a spark,' he thought she said, but already her eyes were closing. She was fast asleep in moments, and a deep, deep silence descended on the ruin.

Adam watched her for a while.

For the first time in a long time, he smiled.

Then he picked up his delivery bag, and went back into the world, alone.

Chapter
Four

Adam walked out onto Tottenham Court Road. It was a shock. Inside the ruined building, it felt like time had stopped. Outside, the modern world rushed by, harsh and loud and brutal. Already, he could smell the city's smoke and grime, so different to the sweet, high scent of the tyger.

He put his head down and made himself get back to work. At once, he felt people's eyes on his skin again. But the memory of the tyger was burning bright inside him. He felt warmer when he thought about her. The rain lashing down on him didn't seem so hard.

He raced through the streets, delivering his parcels, collecting the customers' payments. The last delivery of the day was to a place on the New Road. Only the richest people lived here, in great white mansions set back behind black iron railings. At the end of the road, by the biggest mansion of all, he saw the signs he was looking for, hanging from the railings:

MALDEHYDE'S MENAGERIE
LONDON'S FINEST COLLECTION OF ANIMALS!

The menagerie had three gates. Adam had to go the long way round: past the first class entrance, which was for lords and ladies; past the one for commoners; and finally to the gate for foreigners, at the back. There was a queue outside. Most were tourists from other parts of the Empire, on their Midwinter holidays. They were smiling and laughing under their umbrellas, excited to see the animals.

A gust of wind cut through Adam's coat. He shivered as he sloshed past the people, through the puddles, up to the guards at the gate.

'Delivery from Alhambra & Company, sir,' he said, as he showed a guard his papers.

'Alhamper?' said the guard. Adam gritted his teeth. His name brought him nothing but trouble. 'Oh, I see,' the guard went on, as he took down Adam's details. 'It's *Aaaal-Haaaam-Braaaa!*' he said, dragging out each syllable painfully. 'And your Christian name is Adam?'

Adam looked away, avoiding his gaze, but there was no way he could avoid the question. 'I'm not Christian, sir,' he said. 'I'm Muslim, like my family. But my first name is Adam.'

'Oh,' said the guard. 'Well. You speak good English, for a foreigner.' He opened the gate. 'Go through to that mansion at the end.'

Adam took a deep breath, and went into the grounds, past the colourful signs:

SIR MORTIMER MALDEHYDE WELCOMES YOU TO HIS FAMOUS MENAGERIE!

OUR ANIMALS ARE VERY RARE, AND KEPT HERE FOR THEIR OWN PROTECTION.

DO NOT FEED THEM!

Adam felt colder and colder as he walked through rows of covered cages. Inside them were creatures from every corner of the British Empire: from Africa, India and the Middle East. Even the American Colonies.

There were no tygers, of course. But there was a bear, which was being fed by its keepers as spectators watched in awe. There were monkeys doing tricks: jumping up onto each other's shoulders, then tumbling down as the people laughed. And there was an elephant on a chain, giving rides to children. It was being guided by some men in turbans who were trying to keep their heads down, just as Adam was.

Before he'd met the tyger, he might have been thrilled by this menagerie. But now he couldn't help imagining her in one of those cages, and shuddering at the thought.

He approached the mansion at the end of the grounds. It was the grandest building he'd ever been to, with tall stone columns and intimidating double doors. His hands shook as he reached up to ring the bell.

After a moment, a dark-skinned slave in a butler's uniform opened the doors, and bowed silently. Adam bowed silently back, and gave him the parcel. As the slave handed over the payment, Adam couldn't resist peering over his shoulder, through the doors and into the mansion, where only lords and ladies were allowed.

And just for a moment, he glimpsed cage after cage after cage in there, though he couldn't tell what was inside them. Then the slave closed the doors and Adam walked away, his head down again, and silent as always. All he wanted now was to get out of this place, and go back home.

sniff sniff   sniff sniff

Very carefully, he put his head up to see two bloodhounds by the gate. They were sniffing at everyone who went through, as if searching for a particular scent.

A tourist walked up in front of him. The hounds

24

sniffed her, but let her pass.

Adam's mouth went dry as he came closer. What were they searching for?

The bloodhounds sniffed his boots. Their nostrils quivered.

And then they began to bark.

A man on horseback rode up at once. This man had a pale white face, a white shirt and trousers, and a scarlet coat that stood out like blood on winter snow. These were the clothes of a huntsman. And as Adam looked up, he saw the words *MALDEHYDE'S MENAGERIE* stitched on that scarlet coat.

'I believe my hounds have caught a scent,' the huntsman said, in a voice so sharp and cold, Adam's own blood seemed to freeze. 'Where have you been today, boy? Have you seen the beast?'

Chapter Five

Panic clawed at Adam's chest. The bloodhounds were still barking at him. Everyone in the menagerie was staring as he stood there at the gate, facing the huntsman.

Have you seen the beast? An image of the tyger leaped into his mind: eyes of liquid gold, gazing at him as he promised to keep her secret.

'Something strange is on the loose in London,' the huntsman was saying. 'Something dangerous. Have you seen it?'

Adam's chest was tight. It was getting hard to breathe. But he couldn't betray the tyger.

'No, sir,' he said. 'I haven't.'

The huntsman looked at him harder. Sharper. His

eyes seemed to burn into Adam's brain.

'You *have* seen something,' said the huntsman. 'My hounds can smell it on you. So what was it? Where is it?' He uncoiled a long leather whip, and dangled it from his hand.

At that moment, one of the guards came in from the gate. He was dragging someone behind him. Someone about the same size as Adam, dressed in a cloak and hood that covered their face and hair completely.

'Look what I found, sir,' said the guard. 'She was outside the gates, acting all suspicious. Take that hood off, girl. Let's see your face.'

Slowly, reluctantly, the girl pulled back her hood. Her skin was dark. Her hair was black and braided, and her eyes were bright behind her spectacles.

Adam knew her. It was Zadie True, from the Ghetto. She did the deliveries for her father's shop, as he did for his family. And she was in trouble, just as he was.

The huntsman pointed his whip at her. 'Are you one of Sir Mortimer's slaves?' he said. 'Are you trying to escape?'

'I am no one's slave, sir!' said Zadie, her voice ringing out loud and clear, despite the fear she must have felt. 'I'm a free British citizen, and I have the papers to prove it. And I wasn't doing anything suspicious. I'm just doing my deliveries.'

'You're not delivering anything to this menagerie!' said the guard. 'Admit it. You wanted to see the animals without paying, didn't you?'

Zadie looked down. There was a moment of silence, which grew longer, and longer.

'Um – she was waiting for me,' said Adam. He couldn't just stand there and watch; he had to try and help. 'We're doing our deliveries together today. I had one here, and she didn't, so she was waiting – right, Zadie?'

Zadie looked up and saw him. 'Adam?' she said. A smile spread across her face. 'So there you are! What took you so long?'

The guard grunted, and let her go. But the

huntsman was staring at Zadie.

'If you have been together today,' he said, 'then one of you will tell me what I want to know. My hounds have caught a scent on this boy. The scent of a strange and fearful beast that is on the loose in London. It's vital that you tell me everything you know about it.'

Zadie looked at Adam. He shook his head. The tyger's eyes were still burning at the back of his mind. He had to keep her secret. But – what could he say?

'Oh!' said Zadie, snapping her fingers. 'The dung!' She pointed at Adam's boots. 'Remember?' she said. 'You weren't looking where you were going, as usual . . .'

'. . . and I stepped in a heap of dung!' Adam felt a wave of sweet relief as he saw what she was doing, and played along. 'Of course. We never saw the beast that made it.'

'I wish we had,' said Zadie, turning back to the huntsman. 'It was spectacular! A great steaming heap of dung, and it stank all the way to high heaven! I'll bet that's what your clever hounds can smell.'

The bloodhounds blinked and wagged their tails. The huntsman looked appalled. He cracked his whip at them.

'Dung?' he said. 'You disgusting children – get out

of here, the pair of you, and stop wasting my time!'

They ran. They ran as fast as they could, and didn't say a word to each other until they were far from the menagerie, halfway down Oxford Street, where they had to stop with everyone else for some lords and ladies to ride across the first class lane.

'Thank you, Zadie,' said Adam, as he got his breath back. 'Thanks for that story about the dung. It was brilliant!'

They both burst out laughing. Above their heads, between the buildings, the Midwinter Lights were just coming on. Even higher, in the sky over London, Adam could see the rain easing off at last, and a tiny gap opening in the clouds.

'And thank you for your story about the deliveries!' Zadie was saying. Her eyes sparkled behind her spectacles. 'I owe you.'

Adam shook his head. 'No, you don't,' he said. 'We're even. More than even.'

'Really?' she said. She scratched her head. 'So – was that huntsman right? *Did* you see something strange today?'

Adam chewed on his pencil. Part of him wanted to tell her about the tyger. It was such a big secret to keep to himself. And he liked Zadie. Their paths had often crossed as they went about their work. He'd even been to her father's shop a few times, to make deliveries there.

But he didn't know her nearly well enough to trust her with such a secret. And the tyger's words still echoed in his mind. *My enemy's agents are forever on my trail. Please, tell no one I am here.*

'Why are you acting so weird?' said Zadie. 'Just answer the question!' Then her eyes went wide, and she began to stare at him, like the huntsman had. 'Oh – you did see something, didn't you? You saw the thing that Maldehyde is searching for!'

'What do you mean?' he said, backing away. 'I'm not acting weird!'

The first class lane was clear at last. Everyone else surged forwards to cross the road. But Zadie just stood there, staring at Adam.

'All right,' she said, more quietly. 'Listen.' She came in close, and her voice dropped to a whisper. 'The truth is, I wasn't at the menagerie to look at any animals. I've been watching Sir Mortimer Maldehyde for a long time now, and I need to know what he's after. So if you really did see something strange today – please tell me.'

Adam took another step back from her, into a deep puddle that splashed up over his boots. He looked down to see the Midwinter Lights reflected there in strange distorted shapes. 'Why do you need to know?' he said. 'And – why are you watching a lord, Zadie?'

The gap in the clouds closed again. The sparkle went out of her eyes. 'None of your business,' she said.

'Right,' said Adam defiantly.

'Fine!' said Zadie, as the winter wind whipped around them. She took off her spectacles and wiped the rain away from them. 'Don't tell me what you saw, then. Just tell me where to find it?'

But the more she asked, the less he could say. He felt sure of only one thing. He had to protect the tyger from her enemies – whoever they might be.

He began to run.

'Wait!' called Zadie. 'I can help!'

But already Adam was dashing across Oxford Street, splashing through the puddles, leaving her far behind as he raced back to the Soho Ghetto, alone.

Chapter Six

Adam's pulse pounded as he went through the checkpoint back into Soho. Yet even as he answered the soldier's questions, in his mind all the time was the tyger.

He'd managed to keep her secret from Zadie, as well as the huntsman. But he had to be more careful from now on, and do nothing that might give her away to anyone.

It was a relief to return to the Ghetto, and to see people from all over the Empire around him again. It didn't matter what he looked like here. Even if the Soho streets were narrow, and the crumbling old buildings were black with chimney smoke, this was still his home. The only place foreigners were allowed

to live. And the only place he felt safe.

His family's shop was at the heart of Soho, on the corner of Broadwick Street and Marshall Street. *ALHAMBRA & COMPANY: ALTERATIONS & REPAIRS* said the letters on the window. The whole family worked in the shop, and lived upstairs. And there was his father, chewing on his beard as he waited for Adam by the door.

'Where the devil have you been, boy?' he said, hugging Adam hard. 'I thought something terrible had happened. What took you so long?'

'I got caught in the storm, Baba, and had to take shelter,' said Adam, choosing his words with care. 'But look: I made the deliveries. The payments are all here, see?' He handed over his bag, with the money in it.

'Let's hope so,' said Baba, as he began to count it. 'For all our sakes.'

Adam went into the shop. His big brother Ramzi was working behind the counter. He looked tired, with dark bags under his eyes, but nodded briskly as Adam came in.

'I knew we could depend on you, little brother,' he said. Then he gave Adam a sideways look. 'But you didn't leave the main road and get into trouble, did you?'

Adam's heart thumped. 'Of course not!' he said. 'It was fine.' He couldn't admit that a robber had chased him into the dump, and nearly got him. If he did that, they would worry, and want to know more. And that would risk giving away the tyger.

'The money's all there, thank God!' said Baba. A big smile lit up his face, behind his beard. 'Well done, Adam,' he said. 'I know your job isn't easy. But we all have to work our hardest if we're going to survive.'

Ramzi looked relieved, too. 'So it really went all right?' he said. 'Did the soldier at the checkpoint ask where you were from?'

Adam groaned. That was the question he dreaded; he never knew how to answer it. He turned to his father. 'Baba?' he said. 'What should I say when they ask that? Where *are* we from?'

Baba sighed. 'I've told you before, it's complicated,' he said. 'Your mother and I came here from the Middle East. But you were born in London, and that's all anyone needs to know.'

'That's right, we're Londoners,' said Ramzi, with a grin. 'But Baba – most Londoners are on holiday right now. So can we take the day off tomorrow?'

'You know those holidays aren't for us!' snapped Baba. 'Now go to the back room, both of you, and Mama will tell you about the new job that needs doing tomorrow.'

'What – another job?' muttered Ramzi, his grin fading. Adam could feel walls closing in around him as they left the front room. If he had to do yet another job, how was he ever going to get back to the tyger? And it troubled him that his parents never talked about the places they were from. There was so much more he wanted to know.

The windows of the back room had been bricked up, to save paying the Glass Tax. It was always dark in there. Even with all the lights on, and the coals crackling in the fireplace, it felt almost as dark as the ruined building where he'd met the tyger.

Adam's mother was working here, mending worn-out clothes. His little sister Hana was stacking up the work, ready for Ramzi to pack into parcels for delivery. Paper was expensive, so Ramzi was the only one allowed to touch it. Adam could only gaze at it, even as he chewed on the end of his pencil.

'Hey, Adam?' said Hana. 'Draw us a picture while we work? Something funny, like you used to – I'm so bored in here!'

Adam laughed. It was hard to imagine now, but he'd drawn cartoons for his sister once upon a time, when things were a bit better, and they were still allowed to play as well as work.

'Don't be such a baby, Hana,' said Ramzi, packing up a parcel. 'You know we can't afford to waste paper. He already stole a piece from me today.'

Mama looked up with a strange expression on her face. She'd been embroidering an old shirt with golden thread, creating beautiful patterns that made the fabric look almost new.

'You haven't been drawing again, have you, Adam?' she said. 'Show me.'

Adam's face flushed. He reached into his pocket, and handed her the scrap of paper that had fallen out at the checkpoint; the drawing the soldier had almost seen.

That strange expression on Mama's face grew sharper. She crushed Adam's drawing down to a ball, and threw it in the fire.

'This has to stop,' she said. 'People like us cannot do things like this. Draw one more picture, and you will be punished for it – do you understand?'

Adam stared at the bricked-up windows. He couldn't bring himself to reply. He could only nod in silence as the fire devoured his drawing, burning it down to ash.

'Good,' said Mama. 'Now, we've taken on work for some new customers outside London. Whoever delivers it will have to walk a long way through the common lands north of the city – hard places, far from any roads.' Her needle flashed, and Adam remembered the glint of the robber's knife, and shivered. 'I wish I didn't have to ask you this,' said Mama, more softly. 'But our debts are getting bigger, and we need the money badly, so one of you must do it.'

'I'll do it!' said Hana, so thrilled at the thought, she threw off her hairband, and shook out her curly hair. 'I've heard there's open fields out there, and even animals—'

'You know you're too young, my dear,' said Mama, tying Hana's hair up again. 'No, it must be Ramzi or Adam.'

Hana looked crushed. Ramzi looked exhausted. He kept his head down as he silently wrapped a parcel. It was obvious that Mama wanted him to do this job. But it was equally obvious that he didn't want to.

Adam didn't blame him. It was the most dangerous job they'd ever been asked to do. He'd never even left London before. At the thought of it, he felt his heart begin to race –

– and yet, if he could just do these deliveries fast enough, he could see the tyger. No one would expect him home for hours.

'I'll do it,' he said, surprised to hear the words

39

aloud, as if someone else had spoken. Ramzi looked stunned, like a prisoner who'd just been saved from hanging.

'Are you sure, Adam?' said Mama. She looked at Ramzi, then back at Adam again. 'Well – thank you. It's very responsible of you to volunteer. The first batch must go tomorrow morning to a village called Highgate. It's miles away, so you'd best set out at dawn. And . . . be careful.'

Adam looked at the bricked-up windows again. He could almost see the tyger on the other side. He could smell that sweet, high, honeysuckle scent, drawing him on, despite his fear.

'Be more than careful,' said Ramzi, handing Adam a neatly wrapped parcel. 'And make sure you don't draw on this. Don't do anything that might get you in trouble. Keep your head down, keep your mouth shut, and do what really matters – all right?'

Yes, thought Adam, as the tyger's eyes glowed at the back of his mind. That's exactly what I'm going to do.

Chapter Seven

Adam woke long before dawn. He gulped down a bowl of gruel. Then he threw on his coat, grabbed a map and a delivery bag, and went out into the cold.

It was still dark as he crossed the checkpoint. The soldier took his time today, not only asking questions but also searching Adam's bag thoroughly, examining every parcel before letting him through.

Adam ran on to London's northern limits, by the walls of St Pancras Cathedral, on the banks of the River Fleet. It was so cold, the puddles had frozen over. He shivered, and just for a moment, he hesitated. It was hard enough being a foreigner outside the Ghetto. How bad would it be outside

41

London altogether?

But the memory of the tyger still burned bright inside him. It warmed him and gave him courage as he hurried on, further from home than he'd ever been before.

He followed the river out of the city, north towards Highgate. The streets soon gave way to fields. There were no more pavements to walk on. But there were no more walls or first class lanes, either. It all seemed to be common land, free for anyone to use. So he put his head down and ran through the open fields as fast as he could.

As dawn broke behind the cloud-covered sky, he saw some sheep, grazing on the banks of the river. His sister was right: there really were animals out here!

'Hey! You!' bellowed a huge voice.

He looked up to see two men, both very big and broad, with bushy red hair and beards. They were rounding up the sheep. They must be shepherds. And he had just run through the middle of their flock.

'What is you doing here?' yelled one of them, striding up to Adam. There were twigs in his tangled beard. 'What is you wanting to take from us now? You'll never get the animals, or the land!'

'I don't want to take anything from you!' said

Adam, holding his hands up. 'I'm sorry, sir – I'm just on my way through, doing deliveries for my family's shop.'

The man hollered some terrible curses. Adam's heart thumped. He was in trouble again. And out here in the open, there was nowhere to hide.

He backed away, to the edge of the river. But the shepherd was shouting so loud, he was scaring his own sheep. The flock broke apart. And then –

'*Baaaaaaaa!*'

– a tiny little lamb bolted out from behind him, and ran at the river in panic.

'Lamb!' cried the man. 'No – you'll drown!'

Adam could hear the river rushing past behind him, very fast and cold. But he threw himself to the ground, and managed to grab the lamb before she fell into the icy water.

It was astonishing to hold such a small animal in his hands. She bleated as he stroked her soft white fleece. He could feel her heart beating fast beneath his fingers.

'Ssssh,' he whispered. 'It's all right. No one's going to hurt you.'

The lamb stopped bleating. Her heartbeat slowed. She blinked up at him with trusting eyes as he got back to his feet. And to his surprise, the shepherd was smiling.

'That's . . . very decent of you, lad,' he said. 'Isn't it, Lamb?'

'*Baaa! Baaa! Baaa!*' bleated the lamb. But they were happy bleats this time, like laughter, and Adam couldn't help smiling too as he gave her back to the shepherd.

'God bless you, lad!' the big man said, as he cradled the lamb like a child. 'I is Old Jack, and that there is Big Jackie.' The other shepherd was striding up to join them, bringing the rest of the flock. He was even bigger than Old Jack. And only now did Adam notice that these men had almost nothing, except for their sheep. Though they were dressed in green, their clothes were just scraps of old rags and leaves.

'Sorry if we is scaring you, lad!' said Big Jackie. 'We has to defend the land, see.'

'But – isn't this common land?' said Adam. 'Who are you defending it from?'

Big Jackie dug his feet into the earth. 'Them that wants to take it for themselves,' he said. 'Them that is enclosing the land in fences and walls, to keep the rest of us out.'

'This is the last of the common land,' said Old Jack with a sigh. 'There used to be so much of it, and so many of us, but this is all that's left round here.' He peered at Adam. 'Why don't you stay with us, lad, and help us with the animals?' he said. 'We could use the help. And we may not have a lot, but we is sharing what we got. Give him some breakfast, Jackie!'

The other shepherd grinned. He pulled a bunch of muddy old turnips from his back pocket, and offered them to Adam as if they were the finest food on earth.

'Thank you!' said Adam. 'I wish I could, but I have to get on with my work.' Part of him really did want to stay here, with them. But at the back of his mind, the tyger's eyes were still glowing. He couldn't stop if he wanted to see her again.

'Well, you do whatever you wants, lad,' said Old Jack, chomping into a turnip. 'But next time, maybe look where you is going – eh, Lamby-Lamb-Lamb?'

'*Baaaaaaa!*' bleated the lamb in bliss, as the big men fed her.

The day grew brighter as Adam moved on. He reached the foot of Highgate Hill before noon. The climb was hard, but when he looked back from the top, he had an open view across the fields, all the way to London. Yet to the east and west of the city, there were no more fields. Just the towering chimneystacks of factories and power stations, belching clouds of smoke that filled the sky.

There was one small gap in the clouds, like a crack in the roof of the world. A single shaft of light was streaming through it. Adam wished he could see even higher, past the clouds, into whatever lay beyond. He imagined himself for a moment, flying into an open sky, limitless and free – but forced himself to look down again, and move on.

He made his deliveries around the village quickly. Most of the customers just took their parcels and paid him. But the last delivery of the day was to a grand old mansion, where a slave in a maid's uniform opened the door and bowed silently to him. As Adam bowed silently back, she unwrapped the parcel to check its contents before paying him. And the packing paper fell to the floor.

Adam knelt at once to pick it up for her. She looked horrified. 'No, no, sir!' she pleaded, kneeling beside him. 'That's for me to do!'

'It's all right,' he said, as they stood up together. 'I want to help.' And he gave her the paper with a smile.

It made things worse. She took the paper with trembling hands. For a moment, he thought he saw raw scars, like chains across her wrists, but she quickly turned to look back into the mansion. When she saw no one there, she turned to face him again, shaking. 'You don't understand, sir,' she whispered. 'What they'd do, if they saw . . .'

Adam felt her fear searing into him, deeper than any he'd ever known. He shivered. 'I'm sorry,' he said. 'I didn't mean—'

'But no one saw, thank the Lord,' she went on, touching the cross on her throat. 'And I know you were trying to be kind.' Adam looked down, gazing at the paper he'd just given her. She must have noticed, because when she gave him the payment, she pressed that piece of paper back into his hands. 'Maybe you can find a use for this, sir?' she said quietly. 'It'll only be thrown away as rubbish here.'

'Oh – thank you!' said Adam, as she closed the door. He walked away, stunned, clutching the paper in his hands. He'd never heard a slave speak like that before. They were always silent, speaking only when their owners spoke to them. So he'd done his job in silence too. He never would've said a word if she hadn't spoken first.

Now he wished they could talk much more. But it was impossible. He would never know her name, or hear her story. He would never even be able to thank her properly for the paper.

He folded it and put it in his pocket, his mind full of troubled thoughts. His family had always told him to keep his head down and talk to no one if he wanted to survive. Yet today, he'd seen and heard things that made him wonder if that was right.

And his head was up, looking at the sky, as he made his way back to London, and the tyger.

Chapter
Eight

'Tyger?' called Adam, as he burst into the ruined building at the heart of the dump.

There was no reply.

'Tyger?' he called again. Still there was no reply. As he searched for her in the shadows, he saw no sign of her at all. But he noticed many things he'd missed the day before, when he was running from the robber.

In the first room he walked through, the roof had caved in. It was wide open to the sky. A tree was growing in there, its twisted branches reaching for the light.

In the next room along, deep puddles glimmered on the ground, with drifts of sand all around them.

50

Adam held his breath as he entered the final room, the darkest room. The room where he'd met the tyger.

Silence. Absolute silence. He could hear nothing but his own heart beating. There was not even a trace of her scent in the air. As his eyes adjusted to the darkness, he saw wildflowers growing up from beneath the broken floor. Yet there was still no sign of the tyger.

Had she been captured? Or killed? He should never have left her. Now he'd never see her again.

'Tyger!' he cried. 'Where are you?'

The words burst out of him; he didn't expect a reply. But then the air filled with the sweet, high scent of honeysuckle growing wild. Two points of light appeared, and the tyger emerged from the darkness, her eyes shining like liquid golden fire.

'I am here,' said the tyger. 'I have been here all the while.'

Adam wanted to fling his arms around her in relief. Yet the sound of her voice made him feel strange and shy once more.

'Oh, Tyger,' he said. 'I thought you were . . . gone.'

The tyger rumbled. She padded around the room as if patrolling it: ears sharp, tail flicking, whiskers probing the air. But she was limping. And Adam could see fresh blood on her fur, shockingly wet and red.

'Never fear,' she was saying. 'Tygers were stealthy. They could melt into the shadows, camouflaged by the patterns of their stripes. They could even conceal their scents, or leave scent-trails for others to follow. What kind of world could kill them all? And what kind of future can such a world have?'

'Tyger?' said Adam, chewing on his pencil. 'Why are you talking about tygers like that? And – what do you mean about the world?'

The tyger stared at him, incredibly sharp focus in her eyes. 'There are many things in this world that trouble me,' she said. 'Do they not trouble you, too? The last time you came here, it was in fear for your life.'

Adam remembered the robber, and looked back over his shoulder, to make sure he wasn't there.

'You need fear that man no more,' said the tyger. 'He is far away from here now, and you shall not see him again. I am glad I was able to protect you from him – but this world could be different, and so could you. You could protect yourself, if you learned to use your power.'

'Power?' said Adam. The way she spoke made his head spin. 'What power?'

The tyger's eyes gleamed. She sat up straighter for a moment, and her stripes seemed to widen, like a river flowing out into the sea. 'There is power in you,' she said. 'It is in every single one of you. Enough to change the fate of this world, and more.'

Adam laughed. 'I'm just a boy!' he said. 'A foreigner. What power could I have?'

'The power to help me, if you wished to,' said the tyger quietly.

'Oh!' Adam's heart skipped a beat. 'What can I do to help you, Tyger?'

She turned to lick her shoulder, trying to stop the blood that was still dripping from her wound. Then she gazed up at the window. The creeping vines that grew over it seemed thicker than before. They were closing in, like a net, cutting out the light.

'I am still awaiting the Guardians,' she said. 'Without them, I fear I will not survive. I know they are somewhere in this city. Could you find them, and bring them to me?'

'I could try,' said Adam. 'Who are these Guardians? What do they look like?'

'They are a secret order, sworn to fight beside me in the war.'

'But . . .' Adam looked down. 'How do I find them, if they're secret?'

'By using your power, of course,' said the tyger. 'There are three doors that I may show you. You will find a different kind of power behind each one. But be warned. If you go through these doors, you will see things you might not wish to see; things few mortals ever see. Are you sure you wish to go on?'

Once again, Adam didn't understand everything the tyger was saying. All he knew was that he wanted to help her.

'Of course, Tyger,' he said. 'If you really think I have some sort of power – then show me what it is!'

Chapter Nine

'Tell me,' said the tyger, in the darkness of the ruin. 'What do you see there, on the ground?'

Adam looked at the broken floor, and the wildflowers growing up from underneath. He wanted to help the tyger, but how could this possibly help?

'Do not think about the question,' said the tyger. 'Simply tell me what you see.'

'Wildflowers?' said Adam. 'Just ordinary flowers. Nothing special.'

The tyger's tail thumped. 'Perception is the first of your powers,' she said. 'You were born with it, yet it is locked away inside you. If you wish to release this power, you must open the doors of perception, and go through to the other side.'

She stepped away. And there, in the wall behind her, was a pair of doors.

Adam felt certain they hadn't been there before. And yet there they stood. Double doors, bigger than he was, made of burnished bronze.

He couldn't see what was on the other side. But there was a crack down the middle, between the doors, through which he could see a whisker of light. The brightest light he'd ever seen.

He reached out to touch the doors. They were solid metal, hard and heavy. He pushed on them – and nothing happened. The doors didn't move an inch. And the light through the crack was so bright, it hurt. He held up a hand to protect his eyes.

'That is the light of your own power!' said the tyger. 'Do not turn away from it. Give it everything you have, and you will go into the light.'

Adam braced himself. For the sake of the tyger, he pushed harder, and harder, putting everything he had into a desperate drive. And finally – with a deep, slow, sighing sound – the doors of perception began to move. Inch by inch, the crack between them grew wider, and the doors opened up before him.

And Adam went through to the other side.

Now that he was standing in the light, it didn't hurt at all. He was still in the same room in the abandoned building. Yet on this side of the doors, everything was different. The air was clearer. It was warmer and sweeter. He could only move through it slowly, as if swimming underwater.

There were wildflowers everywhere. Not just a few of them, but fields and fields of flowers, rippling into the distance. But how was that possible?

'Do not look ahead, or behind!' said the tyger. 'Clear your mind of thoughts. Focus on what is here

58

and now, before you – and *perceive*.'

Adam breathed deep. He focused on the wild-flowers in front of him: the ones he'd seen before. And gradually, they seemed to grow more vivid. They began to glow like jewels, shining with impossibly bright colours.

Every detail stood out sharp and clear. He could see each individual petal now. And he saw that every flower was unique. They were all different shapes and sizes, with fine variations between them.

And these flowers were moving. They were opening and closing, making movements so small and slow, he might never have noticed before. His skin prickled as he realized they were alive; just as alive as he was.

He crouched down to touch a purple flower. He felt the softness of its petals, like velvet on his skin. He breathed in its scent: a subtle violet smell that made him smile and smile. It was like a glimpse of paradise.

'These aren't just ordinary flowers, are they, Tyger?' he said.

He turned around, and saw the tyger herself shining in the light. From the tops of her ears to the tip of her tail, every part of her was glowing with golden light, streaming from her in every direction, as if she was its source. And seeing her like that, Adam was filled with a sense of hope. A feeling that everything would be all right, just as long as she was there.

'Nothing is ordinary,' said the tyger. 'Everything is extraordinary. In all of infinity and eternity, that flower exists only in this world; this precise position in space and time. Everywhere else, there is a different flower, or no flower at all. And the same is true of you. Nothing special? You are miraculous beyond measure, both of you.'

Adam turned to look at the fields of flowers ahead of him. And through the fields, far off in the distance – was that another set of doors he could see? Mesmerized, he took a step forwards . . .

'No!' said the tyger. 'Your mortal senses could not yet bear it. Stay here, with perception. Look into your own heart, and perceive what is there instead.'

Adam looked down – and saw a spark of golden flame, burning in his heart.

He was on fire! Shocked, he threw himself back through the doors of perception, and fell flat on the ground on the other side.

The doors vanished. The light faded. The spark of flame disappeared.

There were no more fields of flowers. He was in a

cold, dark, abandoned building, and the tyger was not a being of shining light, but a wounded animal once more.

'You have nothing to fear,' she said, very softly. 'Some mortals cannot bear the light of perception. Some lose themselves in it, and never return. But you have returned with knowledge of your power. Now you may use it whenever you wish. Simply focus, clear your mind of thoughts, and there it will be, inside you.'

Adam breathed deep, cleared his mind – and there it was, as she said. He let it rise, and saw the wildflowers as vividly as before. He saw the tyger shining. Then he risked another glance down at his heart, and saw that spark of flame again, burning very bright.

'Tyger?' he said. 'What is . . . *that*?'

'A spark from the fires of infinity,' she replied.

Adam couldn't stop staring at it. 'Why is it there?'

The light around the tyger rippled, as if in a gust of wind. Yet there was no wind in the abandoned building. It was totally silent and still.

'All human beings have sparks in their hearts,' she said. 'Most neglect the spark, and so it grows dimmer, until it almost dies. It still burns bright in you, but you must learn to use it fearlessly, for it is the source of all your power, and it will help you to survive.' She raised a paw, and the light shimmered around her. 'What do you most love to do?' she said. 'What might help to calm you, if you were afraid?'

Adam thought about it. He thought and thought. 'Drawing?' he said at last. 'I love drawing. But I'm not allowed to do it . . .'

'Next time your perceptions overwhelm you,' said the tyger, 'draw the things you perceive, until you can use this power calmly and clearly. Then you shall know the Guardians, for you shall see the light of their power shining all around them, just as you see it now in me. But please, do it soon. My enemy's agents are coming closer every day.'

Adam shivered. 'These agents,' he said. 'Is there a way to recognize them, too?'

The tyger's tail thumped behind her. 'You shall know them with the same power,' she growled.

'There is no spark inside them. There is nothing in their hearts but one purpose: to capture me. And so they will never stop coming for me, never, not until they succeed, and my enemy wins the war . . . unless you can find the Guardians first.'

Chapter
Ten

Adam knew he had to find the tyger's Guardians. But as he walked out of the ruined building and back through the rubbish dump, he wondered if the power of perception would work, out here in the world, without the tyger to help him.

He focused. He breathed deep; cleared his mind of thoughts. At once, the power rose up inside him. And the world looked very different.

He saw shards of broken glass glinting on the ground like diamonds. He saw crushed tin cans glowing silver in the light. He could feel the wind on his skin; the whole world moving and turning and spinning around him.

All of it was beautiful, and all of it alive.

He glimpsed a reflection of himself in a puddle. He waved at it, and the reflection waved back, as if it was another version of himself. The clouds he could see reflected seemed to be other clouds in other skies. It was like looking into another world.

He gazed at it for a moment in wonder, but made himself walk on. He had to start his search.

He came out onto Tottenham Court Road. He saw the same busy city street he'd always seen. But now he wondered how he'd ever taken it for granted.

Because now every brick in every building, every paving stone and railing, every branch of every tree – everything was miraculous, just as the tyger said. Even the rain that was falling on his head, and the *clop clop clop* of horses' hooves on the first class lane. The most ordinary things had become extraordinary.

Especially the people. For now he could see the sparks of flame that burned inside them. Whether they were rich or poor, old or young, British or foreign – they all had sparks of flame in their hearts, every single one.

Some lords rode down the first class lane on horse-back. Their slaves followed silently behind them. Commoners stood aside to let them pass. They all had sparks in their hearts. There was nothing better about the lords; nothing lesser about the slaves, or the commoners. So how could the lords look down on everyone else? It was like one flower thinking it was better than the rest!

And as he watched, Adam started to see that each individual spark was unique, just like the flowers. He could see everything from the smallest, palest points of light to sparks that blazed like bonfires. It was dazzling.

Yet none of these people were shining with the light of their power, as the tyger had described. None

66

of them seemed to be Guardians.

And as they streamed by, he saw many of them looking back at him, taking in his skin, his hair, his eyes; realizing he was a foreigner. He tried to keep using the power, but the perceptions kept coming, wave after wave, overwhelming –

– so he pushed the power back down, and stumbled into a side street, shaking.

The tyger had told him what to do if this happened. He reached for the piece of paper in his pocket: the one he'd been given on Highgate Hill. He pulled his pencil out from behind his ear, and began to draw what he'd perceived.

One line. Then another. And another, joining them up.

As the lines poured out of him, and a picture started to take shape, Adam felt the happiness he only ever felt when drawing. It was so good to draw again. And it helped, just as the tyger said. He no longer felt overwhelmed.

He let the power rise once more – and looked up to see a man watching him from across the street.

'Hello there!' said the man, beckoning to Adam. He looked friendly, but with the power of perception, Adam could see his spark burning with a violent kind of energy. It was blood red, like a danger sign in his heart.

Adam's throat tightened. Could this man be another robber? He walked rapidly back to the main road – but the man followed him, edging closer, step by step. There was nothing friendly about him now.

Adam walked faster. Heart thumping in his chest, he joined a crowd of people who were all heading in the same direction, hoping for safety in numbers.

And finally, the man gave up, and stopped following him. Adam silently thanked the tyger, for without the power, he would never have suspected the danger.

He stayed with the crowd for a long time, just to be sure. He followed them all the way to St Paul's Cathedral, where many people had gathered in the courtyard, beneath the massive dome. Someone was talking to these people.

A huntsman.

The huntsman from Maldehyde's Menagerie.

Adam's blood twisted. His mouth went dry. He stood stock still at the back of the crowd, trying to stay hidden from the huntsman, who was riding high on his horse, flanked by his hounds. But this time, there was a second huntsman on horseback behind him. And a third. And a fourth.

Four horsemen in scarlet coats, with sharp white

faces; with long leather whips and rifles in their hands. Each one was flanked by a pair of hounds.

Yet Adam could not see a spark in any of their hearts. He saw sparks in all the other people standing beneath the white stone columns of the cathedral – but not in the huntsmen. Their hearts were as cold and empty as the stone.

'The beast escaped from my lord's menagerie,' the first huntsman was telling the crowd. 'You may believe such beasts extinct, but this one is alive and dangerous. If you see it, or hear anything about it, report it at once to Sir Mortimer Maldehyde, at Maldehyde's Menagerie on the New Road. You will be very well rewarded!'

The bells of St Paul's began to ring. Away in the distance, the bells of Bow and Old Bailey were ringing too, as if in reply. The huntsman raised a horn to his lips and blew. The bloodhounds raced away, and the four horsemen rode after them, whips cracking as they galloped down the first class lane.

The crowd was buzzing with excitement at the mention of a reward. Some were already setting off to look for the beast. But Adam could only stand there, heart racing like the horses' hooves. Those huntsmen had no sparks inside them! They must be agents of the tyger's enemy!

If only he knew more about Sir Mortimer Maldehyde. All he knew was that the menagerie belonged to him. That meant he was the one who was really looking for the tyger; the huntsmen just worked for him. So was he also an agent of the enemy?

Then he remembered Zadie True. What was it she'd said, after they'd escaped from the huntsman before? *I've been watching Sir Mortimer Maldehyde for a long time now . . . I can help!*

She seemed to know a lot about Maldehyde. And she definitely didn't like him. Although Adam hadn't trusted her at the time, she clearly wasn't working with the tyger's enemies, but against them.

Maybe he could learn more from her. Maybe he could learn something that would help him keep the tyger secret, and safe, and free.

Chapter Eleven

A dam visited Zadie the very next day.

As he did his deliveries, he kept looking for the Guardians with the power of perception. But as hard as he tried, he could find no sign of the beings of shining light the tyger had described. London was huge; they could be anywhere. He began to fear he would never find them. And all the time, the power within him felt overwhelming.

The moment his deliveries were done, he went to Charing Cross Road: a street on the edge of the Soho Ghetto that was famous for its bookshops. In an alley behind it was Zadie's father's shop. *SOLOMON TRUE & COMPANY: BOOKSELLERS & PRINTERS* said the letters on the window, lit up from inside by a glowing log fire.

Through the glass, Adam could see shelves on every wall, from ceiling to floor. Every shelf was heaped high with books and papers. It was like a treasure cave full of knowledge. He felt sure he would find some answers in there. But he had to get what he needed without giving anything away. So he pushed the power down before he entered the bookshop. He didn't want to be overwhelmed by it in front of Zadie.

He could see her already, working at a big machine, printing some posters. She looked different today. Instead of a cloak and hood, she wore a bright blue dress, and bright blue stockings, too.

Zadie's father Solomon was working behind the counter with paper and pens, laying out more posters for printing. He seemed older than Adam's father. His dark skin was deeply lined. His hair was silver and his clothes were all black, almost like a mourner's. Behind his steel-rimmed spectacles, his expression was very grave.

'Master Alhambra?' said Solomon, as he looked up to see Adam in the doorway, fiddling with his pencil. 'You don't have a delivery for us today, do you?'

Zadie looked up too. Adam blushed and looked down at the ground, where a Persian carpet was

72

spread out, patterned with intricate designs.

'No, sir,' he said. 'I'm here because . . .' He looked at Zadie, and held his hands out wide. 'I'm here because I need your help.'

Zadie smiled at him. 'I'm glad you came,' she said. She went to the fireplace, and put a new log on the fire. 'Look, I'm sorry about what happened last time. Maybe I asked too much. But whatever you need, you really can trust me – and my father.'

Adam smiled back. Something inside him felt warmer and brighter, like the glow of the fire. 'I'm sorry, too,' he said. He took a deep breath. 'I just need to ask you one question. What do you know about Sir Mortimer Maldehyde?'

Solomon looked at the door and shivered, as if the temperature had dropped by ten degrees. 'Why?' he said. 'Is he coming?'

'No!' said Adam. 'Of course not! But – what do you know about him?'

Solomon's spectacles rattled as he laid them on the counter. 'I know he made a fortune in the slave trade,' he said. He rubbed his eyes, and Adam couldn't help noticing there were old, deep scars across his eyebrows. 'He owns land all over the Empire, and many factories, and that menagerie of course . . .' He peered at Adam, and put his spectacles back on. 'But why?' he said. 'Why are you asking?'

Adam chewed on the end of his pencil. 'Um – well – I saw . . .'

'Yes?' said Solomon, as Adam's words tailed away.

'I think he saw something strange,' said Zadie, fanning the flames of the fire. 'One of Maldehyde's huntsmen thought it was the thing they were searching for.'

'Oh!' said Solomon. 'You think he might have

seen . . . Well, what exactly did you see, Master Alhambra?'

They both stared at him from behind their spectacles. And he knew he had to answer the question if he wanted their help.

'Please don't tell anyone,' he whispered. He gripped his pencil tight; so tight, the point dug into the palm of his hand. 'I saw something that shouldn't exist. At least, not in this world. But she does exist, and she's amazing!'

Zadie and Solomon looked at each other in silence, their faces shining in the firelight. Then Solomon started to pull books down from the shelves, laying them open on the counter. And Adam saw they were collections of mythology from all over the world.

'The ancient myths all tell tales of beings who should not exist, and human encounters with them,' said Solomon. 'The tales are so similar, they must surely have some basis in reality. So look closely at these illustrations. They may help us learn more about the being you have seen. Does she resemble any of them?'

Adam's head spun as he leafed through the books. There were pictures of titans and gods, angels and devils, all sorts of strange spirits and mythical beasts. Yet none of them showed a tyger. He shook his head. 'Not exactly,' he said.

'Hmmm,' said Zadie. 'What else can you tell us about her?'

'She's fighting in a war,' said Adam. 'She's been hiding from her enemy. I think Sir Mortimer Maldehyde might be working for this enemy . . .' He paused. 'But is that possible? What do you think, Zadie? Could he be doing something like that?'

'Oh, definitely,' said Zadie, in a very matter-of-fact voice. 'And if he is, then she's in trouble, because

Maldehyde won't stop until he gets what he wants.'

Adam's mouth went dry. But now, from a drawer beneath his counter, Solomon brought out a very old book, bound in finest leather. Stamped on the cover in gold was a picture that took Adam's breath away. A fiery spirit soaring over the minarets and domes of a beautiful city. Zadie went quiet and looked away as her father pointed to it. 'Could this be what you saw?' said Solomon.

'No, sir – but what is it?' said Adam, spellbound.

'One of the djinn,' said Solomon. 'Beings from Islamic mythology: spirits made of smokeless flame who fought a great war with the angels. Do you not recognise this book, Master Alhambra? Did your parents never read you *Alf Layla wa Layla*?'

Adam shook his head. 'Um – what did you just say?'

Solomon smiled. 'It is known in English as *The Arabian Nights*,' he said, 'although it is a collection of tales from all over the Muslim world, not just Arabia. My wife and I grew up reading it, as many Muslims do. She loved it so much, she named our only child after its narrator, Scheherazade – the greatest story-teller of all time.'

Adam was surprised. He'd never realized Zadie was a nickname, short for a Muslim name. He'd never

even realized she was Muslim! And this was the first he'd ever heard of her mother. He hadn't seen anyone else here but Solomon and their customers. Maybe she was working in a back room, like his mother at home?

'Never mind all that, Baba!' Zadie was saying, as Solomon put the book away. 'The only important thing is the being that you saw, Adam. Can you take us to meet her? We need to know more about her if we're going to help.'

Adam hesitated. There was so much he didn't know about Zadie and Solomon. And it was one thing to tell them about the tyger; it was another to take them to see her. If only there was some way to be certain he could trust them . . .

Of course! The power of perception. It was worth a try.

He breathed deep, and cleared his mind of thoughts. And as the power rose up inside him, he saw a spark of golden flame in Zadie's heart, just like his own. There was a spark in Solomon too, burning bright as silver, despite his age.

Whatever their secrets, these people were definitely not agents of the tyger's enemy. Adam had proof of it now. But more than this, as he looked at them, their sparks seemed to be looking back at him;

almost as if they were using the power themselves. He'd never seen such a thing before. The sight was so dazzling, he had to push the power down fast, before it overwhelmed him.

So could Zadie and Solomon be the Guardians? They weren't beings of shining light, as the tyger had described. Yet they weren't the same as everyone else, either. Only the tyger herself could know what this meant.

'I'll ask her,' he said, as he caught his breath, and stumbled to the door. 'I'll go back as soon as I can and ask her for you, I promise.'

'Thank you,' said Zadie. There was a little sparkle in her eyes again as she opened the door for him. 'And – thank you for trusting us. It means more than you can know.'

Chapter
Twelve

Adam ran back through the Ghetto. He passed Turkish coffee shops that filled the air with tempting smells; market stalls where merchants were calling out bargains in every language. He saw temples, mosques and synagogues, as well as churches. It felt like the whole world was here in these streets, and he was always glad to return.

He got home to find his parents had gone out. Ramzi was looking at some new posters on the wall outside the shop. Adam's insides twisted as he read the words:

PUBLIC NOTICE:

THE BEAST IS ON THE LOOSE IN LONDON!

Beneath these words was a terrifying picture. A drawing of a savage, snarling beast, with blood dripping from its teeth. A tyger, but a nightmare of a tyger. Beneath the picture were the lines:

REWARD OFFERED FOR INFORMATION
ABOUT THE BEAST
REPORT TO MALDEHYDE'S MENAGERIE,
THE NEW ROAD, LONDON

'Look!' Ramzi was saying, as Adam stared at the poster in horror. 'This reward could pay off our family's debts! It would change everything if you could find some information about this beast on your delivery rounds.'

Adam took a deep breath, and let the power rise up inside him. He saw the spark in Ramzi's heart burning darkly, like a hot coal; like the smoke that was rising from the chimneys all around them. He stared at the spark, not sure what to make of it. He was sure of only one thing. He could not betray the tyger – not even to his family.

'What's the matter?' said Ramzi. 'Why are you staring at me like that?'

Before Adam could reply, some men walked by the shop, sipping cups of coffee. They looked British, and though their clothes were old, they were made of good cloth. Ramzi immediately turned and bowed to them, sensing the possibility of sales. But Adam sensed something else. He could see the sparks inside them burning with a violent kind of energy: blood red, like danger signs in their hearts.

'Ramzi, no!' he whispered. But Ramzi was already talking to the men.

'Welcome to Alhambra & Company, gentlemen!' he was saying. 'Please, come in. We have some fine new fabrics from Damascus – bargains for you all!'

The men frowned. '*Alhambra?*' said one of them. 'And where are you from, boy?'

Ramzi smiled, though Adam could see his brother's spark was changing, going pale as ash. 'We're Londoners, of course,' said Ramzi. 'Born right here in Soho—'

'No, where are you really from?' said the man, taking a swig of coffee.

'And why are you selling this foreign stuff?' said one of the others. 'Don't you care that British weavers like us can't make a living any more?' He narrowed his eyes. 'Why don't all you cockroaches just get out, and crawl back to wherever you came from?'

They began to walk away. 'Gentlemen, please!' said Ramzi. 'You can't mean that – you're drinking

Turkish coffee!'

Adam's heart was racing. But he could hear his little sister Hana calling to him from inside. He turned and ran through the empty shop, and found her alone in the back room.

'Oh, Adam,' she groaned. 'I'm so bored in here! Mama and Baba never let me out on my own.' She tore her hairband off in frustration. 'Draw me a picture – please?'

Adam exhaled in relief. His heart was still racing, but he knew now that drawing could help with that. And with his parents away, it should be safe, for once. So he pulled his piece of paper from his pocket, and brought his pencil out from behind his ear. Hana clapped her hands in delight, and settled down as Adam began to draw.

One line. Then another. And before he knew it, the lines were pouring out of him, and he was drawing the stripes of a tyger. Not a snarling beast, like that poster outside, but the tyger as he imagined her, in all her power and her glory: a being of pure light, soaring through a distant sky.

Hana watched, the spark inside her burning warm and bright, like molten brass. 'Ohhh!' she gasped, as the picture took shape. 'I love it!'

Adam smiled. Once again, he began to feel the

happiness he only ever felt when drawing. And as he built it up, line by line, he saw that this picture was better than any he'd done before. The more he practised, the better he was becoming. He almost felt as if he was flying himself . . .

. . . until Ramzi burst into the room, bringing him back to earth. 'It's all right, they're gone!' said Ramzi. Then he saw Adam's drawing, and frowned. For a moment, Adam feared his brother would realize he'd seen the tyger, but he just seemed annoyed. 'Am I the only one who cares what happens to this family?' said Ramzi. 'You know you're not allowed to draw! Why can't you do what you're told, instead of wasting time and paper with that baby?'

'Baby?' said Hana. 'I am *not* a baby. You think you're so clever, Ramzi, but you can't even see how grown-up I am!' She stuck out her tongue and waggled her fingers in his face.

'You spoiled brat!' said Ramzi.

He came towards Hana, his hand raised threateningly high. Hana shrieked and began to cry. At once, Adam stood up and put himself between the two of them, protecting his sister with his own body.

'Leave her alone!' he growled. His voice sounded bigger, stronger, almost like the roar of a tyger. 'Leave us both alone. You can't tell us what to do.'

Ramzi rocked back on his heels in shock. Adam had never spoken to him that way before. But with the power of perception, he could see that Ramzi's spark was still as pale as ash – almost as if he was afraid, behind that confident front. And Hana's spark looked like it was about to explode.

'*Maaa-maaa!*' screamed Hana.

Mama burst into the room at that moment, still wearing an overcoat and carrying a cup of coffee. She'd clearly just come home. 'What's all this shouting and screaming?' she said.

'Ramzi was going to hit me!' wailed Hana, rushing up to Mama, making her spill the coffee. 'Adam stopped him, but—'

'She was so rude!' said Ramzi. 'And Mama, he was—'

'Enough!' said Mama, bending to clean up the coffee. 'Don't we have enough trouble, without you turning on each other?'

She stood up again, and started to tie Hana's hair back into the hairband. As she did so, Adam saw something strange in his mother's heart. Not so much a spark as an ember. It was like the end of a fire that was exhausted and burned out. The sight of it made him feel cold.

'I have good news,' said Mama. Her voice was

bright, despite what Adam could see, so he pushed the power down. It was too confusing. 'We've found someone who might help us with our debts,' said Mama. 'He's one of our customers; a generous one. He's even giving us tickets to see the Midwinter hangings at Tyburn! But we won't take you if you behave so irresponsibly.'

'I *was* being responsible!' spluttered Ramzi. 'And Mama, he was drawing! He's forbidden to draw, you said it yourself—'

'I said *ENOUGH*!' yelled Mama, with a strange expression on her face. 'Get out of here, the lot of you, and pray to God that this customer helps us, or you'll see what trouble really is!'

'Just make sure you do what I told you, little brother,' whispered Ramzi, as they left the room. 'I doubt this customer is really going to help us. But if you can find some information about that beast – we can claim the reward for our family!'

Chapter
Thirteen

Adam was up before dawn again the next day. He wanted to go straight to the dump to see the tyger. But he had to make more deliveries north of London first: this time to a village called Hampstead, by the source of the River Fleet.

His head was up as he followed the river through the open fields again. He was taking in all the sights and sounds with the power of perception. So this time, he saw the shepherds and their sheep from a distance, and waved to them.

'Old Jack!' he called. 'Big Jackie! How's Lamb today?'

The shepherds waved back, but they looked worried. As Adam got closer, he began to hear a hard, heavy, hammering sound. It was coming from the next field along, where some people in uniforms were pounding fence-posts into the ground. And now Adam saw official-looking signs had gone up around these fields:

PRIVATE PROPERTY – NO PUBLIC ACCESS
THIS LAND IS TO BE ENCLOSED

'It's happening, lad,' said Old Jack. He huddled into his rags, and hugged Lamb tight and close. 'They is taking all the land.'

Adam shivered. The world felt colder, and smaller, too. 'How can they do that?' he said. 'This is common land.'

'And we tried to defend it,' said Big Jackie, his red beard bristling like broken twigs. 'But it belongs to some lords now, not the likes of us any more. You'll have to go the long way round to get where you is going.'

'*Baaaaaaaa?*' bleated Lamb: a very small, scared-sounding bleat.

'I don't know, Lamb,' said Old Jack, stroking her soft white fleece. 'I don't know where we is going, or what we is doing now.'

Adam shook his head helplessly. Then a terrible

thought cut through his mind, like the wind cutting through his coat. The rubbish dump was common land too. What if someone enclosed it, and stopped him from seeing the tyger?

It was hard to leave the shepherds again, but he had to move on. He said a hurried goodbye, then made his way to Hampstead as quickly as he could. As soon as his deliveries were done, he ran all the way back to Tottenham Court Road, back to the gates of the dump.

He could see no new signs here, though. It was the same as ever: a city block of common land that was public property, open to all, as it always had been. Adam stood outside for a moment, gasping with relief. Then he ran into the dump, through the little wooden doorway into the ruined building. The smoke and grime of the city fell away, replaced by the sweet, high scent of honeysuckle growing wild.

He found the tyger easily this time, in the second room of the building. He smiled to see her curled up by a puddle, her face behind her paws. But as he approached, he saw that her shoulder was still bleeding.

'Tyger?' he whispered, shuddering at the sight.

No reply.

'Tyger!' he said.

The tyger raised her head. Her eyes still glowed like golden fire, though their light seemed fainter than before. She yawned an enormous yawn, and stretched out all four paws. Adam wanted to reach out and stroke her shaggy fur, but he held back. Her sheer physical presence still took his breath away.

'Oh, Tyger,' he said. 'Are you all right?'

'Doubt anything you like,' said the tyger, fierce and proud. 'Doubt the clouds in the sky, the movements of the tide, or the turning of this world around its sun. But never, ever doubt me.'

Adam bit his lip. He knew she must be making a huge effort for his sake, ignoring a wound that wasn't healing.

'You were right about your enemy's agents, Tyger,' he said. 'They're out there, on your trail. I saw them: strange huntsmen with no light inside them, led by someone called Sir Mortimer Maldehyde. They're offering rewards for information about you!'

The tyger gazed up at the window. Adam followed her gaze. The creeping vines that grew across it had closed in, completely blocking out the sky. The tyger's pupils expanded, until her eyes were great pools of liquid darkness, with just a hint of golden fire in their depths.

'My enemy has been hunting me across the worlds

for aeons,' she said. 'He has used many mortals to do his will. He has appeared to them in many forms, and been known by many names himself, though I have always known him as *Urizen*.'

Adam felt dizzy as he tried to imagine this enemy. 'Why is he hunting you?' he said.

The tyger did not reply. She was still gazing up at the window. 'Did you find the Guardians?' she said.

'I don't think so,' said Adam, 'but I did find something strange. I was talking to some people who know a lot about Maldehyde, and I saw that their sparks were different from everyone else's. It felt like they were looking back at me.'

'Ah!' The tyger's eyes gleamed. The puddle glimmered on the ground beside her. 'Then they too have opened the doors of perception. They might indeed be Guardians.'

'But they weren't shining with the light of their power, like you told me,' Adam went on, 'so I wasn't sure if they were the right people. Sometimes, when I'm using perception, I can guess what people are feeling, but I never know what they're thinking, or what they really want. Can you ever know those things?'

'Not with the power of perception,' said the tyger. She looked down into the depths of the puddle.

93

'However, there are other doors that I may show you; other powers that may help you learn the things you wish to know.'

Adam remembered the doors he'd glimpsed in the distance, last time. 'You mean – I need to open the next set of doors?' he said. 'The ones you warned me not to go near?'

The tyger raked her claws through the sand on the edge of the puddle. 'I would never ask you to do anything against your wishes,' she said. 'The deeper you go, the greater the powers, but the greater the dangers, too. The choice must be yours alone.'

A great wave of feeling surged up from somewhere inside Adam. And this time, he couldn't stop himself. He threw his arms around the tyger, and hugged her tight and close. So close, he felt her shaggy fur upon his face.

'I want to do it!' he said. 'I want to help you, Tyger. Show me how.'

She rumbled with surprise. Then she licked his face with a tongue that was rougher than sandpaper, yet softer than velvet.

'I thank you,' said the tyger. 'I thank you, my courageous friend.'

Chapter Fourteen

The tyger reached for the puddle that glimmered on the ground beside her in the ruin. With her claws, she picked out a single grain of sand from its edge.

'Perception can only show you things from your own point of view,' she said. 'But with the power of imagination, you can see from other points of view. People, places, even grains of sand – if you can imagine what it is like to be them, and see from their perspectives, you may find a deeper kind of understanding.'

Adam stared at the tyger. 'How can you imagine being a grain of sand?' he said.

'You must put yourself aside,' said the tyger. 'You

must go through the doors of imagination, to the other side.'

She stepped away. And there, in the wall behind her, was a new pair of doors, where there had been no doors before.

These doors were much bigger than the doors of perception. And this time, they were not made of bronze. They were made of silver.

But once again, there was a crack down the middle, through which he could see a whisker of light. The sharpest light he'd ever seen. It was stabbing into his eyes.

Adam squinted as he reached out to touch the silver doors. He pushed on them as hard as he could – but nothing happened. The doors didn't move at all. And the light through the crack was getting sharper and sharper, slicing his whole body open like a knife.

'I can't open these doors, Tyger!' he said.

'It is not the doors of imagination you must open,' said the tyger. 'It is yourself. So open up your self, and let the light come in. Give up your eyes, and you will see. Give up that limited body of flesh and blood; you cannot take it with you.'

Adam didn't understand all things she was saying – but he did trust the tyger. So he bit down on his teeth, and let the light pour into him despite the pain as it penetrated his eyes, his body, his heart and mind.

And even as it cut him open, it released something deep inside him. He seemed to be rising up, out of his body . . .

. . . going through the crack between the doors . . .

. . . to the other side.

And now there was no pain. He could even see his own body from the outside! It was strange to see it standing there, behind him. But he could move more easily without it, and he could see more clearly, too.

He was still in the same room, in the ruined building. Yet on this side of the doors, everything was different. Instead of walls, there were mountains in the distance. Where there had been puddles, now there were lakes, rivers and streams, with great sandbanks on their shores.

The tyger stood beside him, shining in the light, a grain of sand on the tip of her claw. 'Good!' she said. 'Now go into this grain of sand – and become this grain of sand!'

Adam didn't think twice. He felt so light and free, he could go anywhere. So he dived right into the sand.

It was strange. Dizzying. Disorientating. But his own feelings faded, and he became as small and still and silent as the sand. He was not perceiving it any more. He had become it.

'Now you see what the sand sees,' said the tyger, 'and you feel what it feels. But you can go even deeper. With the power of imagination, you can see everything it has ever seen, for all things leave traces in time. Follow those traces, wherever they may lead.'

Adam kept going, deeper and deeper into the sand. As he went, time seemed to turn and flow backwards. And he began to catch glimpses of other times; echoes of the sand's history, as if it was his own.

He saw the seasons passing. Winters, springs, summers, autumns. Year after year went by. Decade after decade. Century after century.

He saw that this ruined building had once been part of a bigger, grander structure. He heard the ring of trumpets as knights jousted by its walls, while lords and ladies cheered. He saw all the other people who had been here before him, right back to ancient times. Normans, Saxons, Vikings. Romans and Celts, and people even older.

'The grain of sand has been here all this time,' said the tyger. 'This is what it saw. Every one of those mortals came here from elsewhere to conquer this land. And the same thing they did to the land, they did to the animals, and to each other.'

The waves of people kept coming, like tides upon a beach. Adam saw them washing up from Europe, Asia, Africa. Each had different coloured skin, and hair, and eyes.

A forest surrounded him now: trees as far as he could see. People were walking down a path between the trees . . .

. . . and then there were no people. As he went back through time, further and further, faster and faster, ice sheets advanced and retreated, carrying the grain of sand to this spot, and depositing it here.

Adam and the tyger followed the sand through glaciers, rivers and seas, all the way across the world, back to the moment when it had crumbled from a mountain. They saw the mountain being made. Saw rocks created on the ocean floor, layer by layer over millions of years.

Continents and oceans were flowing into new shapes, as if the world itself was one great being, breathing in and out as it turned through time and space. And as meteors began to fall, Adam started to rise up into the sky –

'No!' said the tyger. 'Your mortal senses could not yet bear to leave this world behind!'

– and they fell out of the sand at last. Adam returned to his own body, to the ruined building, to his own time and place again.

It was a shock to be back. He had lost himself completely in the sand. He might never have returned at all. A wave of nausea washed through him at the thought, and he began to shake.

But the tyger was rumbling happily: a sound so deep, it could have come from the bottom of the sea. Adam held on to her like a shipwrecked sailor, warming himself on the heat that was streaming from her heart. And though he was still shaking, his heart filled with pride when he heard her words.

'You did well,' she said, licking his face as if he was a cub. 'Now you can do more than survive in this world. You can begin to understand it, and everyone in it, if you learn to use this power without me by your side.'

'Without you?' Adam's pride drained away. He'd felt so sure that he could help the tyger. Only now was he beginning to see how difficult this might be.

'Perhaps it is too much, too soon,' sighed the tyger. 'If a grain of sand is hard for you, another person will only be harder. But . . . you have more power than you know.' She looked at him like no one had ever looked at him before, with such trust in her eyes. 'So please, go now and practise this. And if the people you have seen are indeed the Guardians, then bring them here to me.'

Adam wanted to be worthy of her trust. So he hauled himself up, though his legs felt weak as water. 'I'll try,' he said. 'If you really believe I can do this – then I will try my best for you, Tyger.'

Chapter
Fifteen

Adam was still shaking as he left the dump. He wasn't ready to use the power of imagination.

But there were posters of the tyger all the way down Tottenham Court Road. *THE BEAST IS ON THE LOOSE IN LONDON!* they screamed. There was no time to waste. However hard this was – he had to do it.

He let the power rise. He left his body, and went into the street. The concrete pavement fell away, revealing an old path underneath. Buildings flickered and faded.

It was dizzying. Disorientating. It was more than he could take, without the tyger. So he pushed the power down, and came crashing back into his body with a sickening jolt. Another wave of nausea washed through him –

– and with a great heave, he threw his guts up all over the pavement. Some people stepped around him sharply, as if he had the plague. Others offered him help. He fled from them all, and stumbled on through the streets, ashamed.

There were more posters of the tyger on Charing Cross Road. Giant billboards of the beast loomed over Leicester Square and Piccadilly Circus. Crowds of people were pointing up at them, talking with great excitement about the reward. Somehow, Adam made his way through them, and back to the bookshop.

'Master Alhambra!' Solomon caught him at door, and helped him to the fireplace. 'Are you all right?'

Adam tried to warm himself by the fire. 'I – I'm not sure, sir,' he said, still shaking. With the power of perception, he could see the sparks in Solomon and Zadie, burning silver and gold as before. But he couldn't use the power of imagination on them. It was just too hard.

Zadie was standing by the printing machine. She was looking at a poster. A poster of the tyger, like the ones he'd seen outside.

'So is this it?' said Zadie, pointing at the picture. 'Is this what you saw?'

103

'She's nothing like that beast!' Adam blurted out. The words exploded out of him before he could stop them. 'Are you the ones who are making those posters for Maldehyde?' he said. 'Or – are you the Guardians?'

It was all out in the open now. Zadie and Solomon stared at him.

'We would never work for that slave trader!' said Zadie. 'I just found this poster on the wall outside. And as for Guardians . . .'

She turned to her father. He was studying Adam quietly from behind his steel-rimmed spectacles.

'It's all right, Scheherazade,' he said. 'He has trusted us with his secret. I think we can trust him, too?' Zadie took a deep breath – and then nodded. 'Good,' said Solomon. 'Follow me, please, Master Alhambra.'

He closed the bookshop, and led Adam and Zadie into a back room. It was small and modestly furnished, with a prayer mat on the floor, and a pot of Turkish coffee on the stove. There was no sign of Zadie's mother. But there was a window that wasn't bricked up, and there were pictures on the wall of a beautiful city, with buildings made of sculpted earth.

'That is Timbuktu, in West Africa,' said Solomon. 'A city of scholars, where the university is older than

Oxford or Cambridge. It's where my wife and I were born, were educated, and then trained at an institution even older. For we were part of an ancient order which believed a great war was being fought over the world by immortals, like the mythic wars of titans and gods, angels and djinn. Members of this order were known as Guardians.'

'I knew it!' said Adam, as Zadie poured out three cups of coffee, and passed them round. Solomon drank his coffee in one deep draught, and went on.

'There were Guardians of every faith and culture,' he said, 'all united to fight beside the immortals who defended humanity in the war. These Guardians were taught a series of disciplines that gave them great powers. Powers of perception, and imagination . . . and there were more, I believe, but we never completed our training.'

Adam's mind was racing as he sipped the coffee. It was scalding hot and bitter, and it burned his tongue. 'Why not?' he said. 'What happened?'

'Slavery,' said Solomon. The word hung in the air as he took off his spectacles, and rubbed the scars across his eyebrows. 'Before we could learn the greatest secrets, we were kidnapped, enslaved, thrown into the pit of a slave ship and taken over the water to a distant land. Many died in that ship. Even those who survived lost everything: our families, our freedom, even our names, for the slavers could not pronounce *Suleiman Traoré*, and so I became Solomon True.'

Adam stared at him, stunned. This was not what he'd expected. He'd never even realized Solomon had once been a slave.

'I was forced to work brutally hard for no pay or purpose but to enrich my owners,' said Solomon. 'They treated me as a thing to be bought and sold, whipped and worse if I said a word. Finally, I was bought by a lord who loved learning, and thanks to my education, I rose to become his secretary. When he died, he freed me, and my child. But my wife –' his voice cracked '– she did not survive. She died when our daughter was just a baby.'

Zadie looked out of the window at the darkening sky. Adam held his head in his hands. There were more secrets here than he'd suspected, and a sense of loss more painful than anything he'd ever known.

'I'm sorry,' he said, though the words were like ashes in his mouth. 'I'm so sorry.'

Solomon seemed unable to speak. Gently, Zadie laid a hand on her father's shoulder.

'I never knew my mother,' she said. 'But my father's given me a good life, despite everything. I wouldn't want to be anyone else's daughter.'

Solomon put his spectacles back on, covering his scars. 'I have done my best,' he said, in a steadier voice. 'But you see, Master Alhambra – once we were taken from Timbuktu, we lost all contact with our order. Many years have passed, and I never heard from them again. I do not even know if there are Guardians in this land.'

'There must be,' said Adam. 'The tyger thinks they're somewhere in London, and she needs me to find them.'

107

'Oh?' Solomon's eyes lit up for a moment. Then he turned away, and gazed at the pictures of Timbuktu on the wall. 'Well, I am not sure how we can help you.'

'But Baba!' said Zadie. 'This is what you and Mama trained for. And it's why you trained me, too. It's why I was out there all that time, using the power of perception, searching for clues. When I told you Maldehyde's huntsmen had no sparks, and must be part of the war of the immortals, you wouldn't do anything, because we were alone. Now someone else knows! And if it's true – if an immortal is really here, in London – we have to help her, don't we?'

Adam's skin tingled as he realized Zadie had the same power as him. He wondered if she could see his secrets with the power of imagination, and blushed at the thought.

Solomon was shaking his head. 'I wish we could be the ones to help the immortal,' he said. 'But she needs the Guardians. Not us.'

Zadie turned to Adam. 'What *does* she need, anyway?' she said, her eyes bright with curiosity behind her spectacles.

'Um – well, she's wounded,' said Adam. 'Maybe these Guardians know how to heal her? She said she wouldn't survive without them.'

'Such knowledge is far beyond us,' said Solomon. 'But . . . perhaps my daughter is right. If there truly are Guardians in London, perhaps I can help you to find them. I will try. In the meantime, will you take Scheherazade to see the immortal? We must learn more about her, and establish exactly what she needs.'

'Of course,' said Adam. He glanced out of the window. The first streetlights were just coming on, lighting up the darkness that was gathering outside.

Zadie smiled. 'That's more like it!' she said. 'We'll figure this out together, and find a way to help her. Can we go and see her soon?'

Adam felt the spark inside him glowing brighter, like the streetlights; a secret glow in his heart. It was so good to know he was not alone any more. 'It's too late today,' he said. 'I have to get home. But meet me tomorrow at noon by the entrance to the dump off Tottenham Court Road, and we'll go from there together.'

Chapter Sixteen

Adam ran all the way home. He felt a new sense of hope after talking to Zadie and Solomon. Although they weren't Guardians, they were going to help him find the Guardians. And together, they would surely find a way to help the tyger.

But when he got home, he found something so strange, it stopped him in his tracks.

A magnificent white horse was tethered outside his family's shop. It had a jewelled saddle and reins, and it was being groomed by some silent slaves. He'd never seen anything like it in the Ghetto before.

He looked through the window, through the words *ALHAMBRA & COMPANY*, into the shop. There was a lord inside: a tall, thin man with a pale white face, dressed in a top hat and tailcoat. He was wearing spectacles with lenses so dark, Adam couldn't see his eyes. But his clothes were cut from the most expensive silk.

Around him, slaves were carrying bales of cotton into the shop, their heads bent low beneath their burdens. Adam's father was listening to the lord, his head bent almost as low.

'. . . pure white cotton from my plantations in the Colonies!' the lord was saying, in a voice as smooth as the silk he wore.

'Thank you, my lord!' said Baba. 'Thank you for your generosity.' He bowed down, and kissed the man's hand. Then he called to the back room, and one by one, Adam's mother, brother and sister appeared. And they all bowed down to kiss the man's hand.

The man inspected each of them in turn, and shook his head every time. But as his slaves left the shop, he saw Adam standing by the window. 'And who is that fine young fellow?' he said.

'Adam?' said Mama, waving to him. 'Come in! Come and kiss the hand of the man who is saving our shop!'

As Adam walked past the shivering slaves and into the shop, he let the power of perception rise up inside him. And his throat tightened, like he was walking into a nightmare. For he couldn't see this lord the way he could see other people. He couldn't see a spark in his heart, yet it was stranger than that. He couldn't see *anything*. It was as if the air was distorted around the lord.

'What are you waiting for?' said Baba, forcing Adam forwards. 'Kiss his hand!'

The man held out a hand for Adam to kiss. His pale white skin felt cold as ice. Adam's own skin began to crawl. But finally, Baba was satisfied, and let him go.

Ramzi pushed Adam aside, and knelt down before the man. 'How can we repay you, my lord?' he said.

'There is just one small thing I would like,' replied the man. 'I should very much like to talk to this brother of yours.' He turned to look straight at Adam, who could feel the power of his gaze, though the man's eyes were still hidden behind the dark lenses of his spectacles.

'Oh!' said Ramzi. 'Well, if that's what you want . . .'

He stood up and dragged Adam back towards the lord. Baba bit down on his beard.

'Adam is just our delivery boy, my lord,' he said. 'He doesn't know anything.'

'Is that so?' said the lord. Outside the shop, some-where in the distance, a church bell began to ring. 'I am sure he has seen all sorts of things whilst making his deliveries. And he is dying to tell us about them – aren't you, young man?'

Adam stood there, cheeks burning as he tried to use the power of perception. But the whole world seemed to be distorted around this lord. Even Baba and Mama were affected.

He could barely see the sparks inside them at all. They were so faint, like the final embers of a fire that was dying, dying, all light and heat extinguished.

'Adam!' said Mama sharply. 'Answer Sir Mortimer when he talks to you!'

Sir Mortimer? At the sound of the name, the blood drained from Adam's face.

'This is Sir Mortimer Maldehyde,' said Baba. He put his arm around Adam, and whispered urgently in his ear. 'He's just taken on our debts! We owe everything to him now, so for God's sake, tell him what he wants to know!'

Away in the distance, bell after bell was ringing, tolling out the time. But Maldehyde spoke to Adam in that silky voice as if there was nothing else in the world.

'You must have seen my posters,' he said. 'A savage wild animal has escaped from my menagerie. I think you might not have told my huntsman everything you know about this beast. So tell me now, and perhaps I will forgive your family's debts to me.'

Excitement crackled through the shop. Everyone stared at Adam. He couldn't meet their eyes. His mind was reeling from the realization that he hadn't escaped from the huntsman after all. He must have told Maldehyde about Adam. And now Maldehyde himself was here, in Adam's home.

If only he could use the power of imagination, he might be able to find out more about this lord. But he couldn't even use perception. All he could do was keep his promise to the tyger.

'I don't know anything, sir,' he managed to say, though it took all his courage to do it.

'Tell me the truth now, boy,' said Maldehyde, with a smile.

His gaze held Adam in an iron grip. Adam wished he could run and hide. But there was nowhere to run. Nowhere to hide. He stood there, trapped, trying with all his might to protect the tyger. With every moment, he felt more helpless and small. But somehow, he held on – held on – held on –

– until at last, Maldehyde turned to face the rest of the family.

'What a stubborn little chap!' he chuckled, as the last church bell tolled, and silence fell outside. 'Well, if any of you can make him talk, do come and see me. I can give you everything you've ever wished for, if you help me find the beast. Otherwise . . .' He looked at the shop window. '*Alhambra,*' he said. 'What an interesting name. Wasn't there once an artist with that name?'

Mama and Baba stared down at the ground in

silence.

'I'm sure that was nothing to do with you,' said Maldehyde. 'You seem like very fine people. But you are foreigners nonetheless, and with debts like yours . . . well, I dread to think what might happen if you couldn't repay them.'

He was still smiling as he left the shop, singing a popular tune:

'Oranges and lemons, say the bells of St Clement's!
You owe me five farthings, say the bells of St Martin's!'

He mounted his horse and rode away, followed by his slaves. Adam's parents watched him go, still speechless.

'Don't worry,' Ramzi told them, the moment Maldehyde was gone. 'I think I know how to find that beast, and save us from our debts.' His spark burned like a hot coal inside him as he turned on Adam, backing him into a corner. 'You were drawing something strange yesterday. Now I understand – it was this beast, wasn't it? You know where it is!'

'You were *drawing*?' said Baba, snapping out of his silence at last. He grabbed Adam's wrist, and dragged him down to the basement of the shop. 'Enough is enough! I am going to get the truth out of you, and teach you a lesson you will never forget!'

Chapter Seventeen

The basement beneath Alhambra & Company was a cold, dark place, filled with old boxes and suitcases. Adam was locked in, and Baba was shouting furiously in his face.

'Why in God's name were you drawing again?' he yelled. 'We've warned you so many times!'

Adam could not reply.

'Is Ramzi right?' demanded Baba. 'Have you seen the beast on those posters?'

An image of the tyger leaped into Adam's mind. She was bleeding, in pain, with no one to help her. And he was trapped in here, powerless and alone.

'And why wouldn't you talk to Sir Mortimer Maldehyde?' Baba went on. 'What the devil is going on, Adam? I am not letting you out of here until you tell me the truth!'

Adam had never seen his father so angry. But though it shook him to the core, at the back of his mind all the time was the tyger. He was desperate to return to her before her enemies hunted her down. What could he say that might convince Baba to let him go?

Then a thought flashed into his mind. Maybe he wasn't powerless. There *was* something he could try. He had to, for the tyger. So he took a deep breath, and let the power of imagination rise up inside him. And before he could change his mind, he went out of his body, and into his father.

It was dizzying. Disorientating. He seemed to be becoming his father, the way he'd become the grain of sand: seeing what he saw, feeling what he felt. But he kept going, determined to find what he needed.

And now, for the first time in his life, he thought he could see what lay behind his father's anger. It was fear. Baba was scared that the family would lose their shop, their money, their lives. He was terrified of being in debt to people like Maldehyde; being bankrupted, kicked out of the country, even hanged at Tyburn.

These fears had nearly extinguished Baba's spark.

That was why there was just a tiny ember left inside him, dying in a vast pit of darkness. And in that pit, there were fears even older and deeper. Memories of terrible violence and destruction.

Adam had only just glimpsed them when a strange new light began to rise up before him. A diamond light that was like all other lights combined. A light so devastatingly powerful and bright, he felt sure it would destroy him. In panic, he pulled away from it, and from his father, and came back into himself.

Once again, it was a shock to return to his body. Nausea washed through him, and he fell to the floor, heaving.

'Adam?' said Baba. 'Are you all right? I didn't mean to scare you like that.'

Adam gathered himself. He was still dizzy and disorientated. But he knew what to say now: the words his father wanted to hear.

'I'm sorry, Baba,' he said. 'I shouldn't have drawn that picture. It was a waste of time and paper. I'll never do it again – I just want to get back to work.'

Baba held out a hand and pulled him back up. 'You're a good boy, Adam,' he said. 'I know you always do your best to help, even if you're afraid. But I need to be certain of something before I let you go, because so much depends on it. Is your brother right?

Do you know *anything* about that beast?'

Adam shook his head. 'I've never seen anything like the beast on those posters,' he said. That, at least, was true.

'I didn't think so,' sighed his father. 'And while Sir Mortimer has been generous, I didn't like his threats one bit. We must work harder than ever to pay back the money we now owe him. So rather than coming with us to see the Midwinter hangings tomorrow, will you do a special delivery instead?'

'Yes, Baba,' said Adam, with a secret flush of relief. He'd forgotten about the hangings. He didn't want to see them anyway. He just wanted to see the tyger.

'We've done a job for a workhouse,' said Baba. 'They've paid us; all you have to do is deliver the clothes. But be very careful. Workhouses are places where the poorest people of this land end up. And when people get desperate, they tend to take it out on foreigners, and followers of other faiths, like us.'

Something in Adam's head began to spin. 'Baba?' he said. 'Please don't get angry, but I really need to know. Where is our family from, originally?'

Baba stared at him in silence for a while. Then he turned to the boxes that were hidden down there in the basement. 'All right,' he said. 'I hoped I'd never have to burden you with this, but you have to understand why it's important to be careful.'

He opened one of the boxes, and pulled out some dusty old paintings. They showed cities in ruins: bullet-riddled buildings, collapsing bridges, shattered minarets and domes. Streets heaped with bleeding bodies. Animals and people, dying.

On the top of each painting was a word in a language Adam didn't know, with a word in English underneath. *Beirut. Baghdad. Damascus.*

Adam found it hard to look away from these pictures. They were so powerful, and so much like the memories he'd glimpsed in his father's mind. But Baba put them to one side. From another box, he pulled out a globe with a map of the world on it. All the lands of the Empire were painted red, so most of the earth was red.

Baba ran his hands in a great sweep over Asia, Africa, Southern Europe. 'I believe our ancestors lived in all these places,' he said. 'People used to move freely around the Muslim world. There are many things I don't know; a lot of our history has been lost and forgotten down the centuries. But I do know your mother and I were born in the Middle East.'

'What does that mean, though?' said Adam. 'Where is the Middle East, exactly?'

'At the heart of the Muslim world,' said Baba,

pointing east of the Mediterranean Sea. 'I grew up there, speaking Arabic. Many Christians and Jews lived there too. Islam, Christianity and Judaism all started there, and they all believe in the same God. Sadly, not everyone sees the similarities. Our lands were torn apart by wars, famines and plagues, until they were conquered by the Empire. Life became very dangerous for us then, as you can see from your mother's pictures.'

'Those are Mama's pictures?' said Adam. He stared at the paintings in shock. 'But – she hates it when I draw!'

'She was the artist Maldehyde mentioned,' said Baba. 'She wanted to show people what it means to be conquered. The Empire doesn't just conquer; it destroys, pollutes, enslaves. Why do you think so many animals are extinct? But she got in terrible trouble for these pictures, and was released only when she agreed to give up painting forever.'

For a moment, Adam thought the spark in his father's heart had gone out completely. Then Baba cleared his throat, and very carefully and gently put the paintings back into their box. He spun the globe once more, tracing a route north and west to London. And a tiny bit of light returned.

'We came here hoping to give our children a

better life,' he said. 'We did all we could to fit in, even giving you Muslim names that could also be Christian names, British names. We never taught you about your history, language or faith, because we thought that would be safest. Yet you are still seen as foreigners too. That's why you must work hard, keep your heads down, and never do *anything* that draws attention, because attention is dangerous. Art is dangerous. Do you understand me now?'

Adam nodded. His whole body seemed to be spinning with a sense of loss for things he'd never even known. But there was no time to say more, because already Baba was walking away from the basement, leaving the door wide open behind him.

It took Adam a moment to realize that he'd done it. He'd used the power of imagination, and persuaded his father to let him go.

It didn't feel like a victory. He didn't ever want to use that power on another person again. He felt sure the diamond light he'd seen would destroy him if he did.

But at least he was free now to go and see Zadie – and to take her to see the tyger.

Chapter Eighteen

A cold white mist hung over London the next day. Midwinter was very close now, and there was almost no light in the sky. Frost lay thick on the ground.

As Adam walked through the streets, he thought he heard footsteps in the frost behind him. He turned to look, but could see no one there. Even so, he couldn't shake the sense that someone was following him.

He passed through Trafalgar Square on his way to the workhouse, and gazed at the grand art galleries by Nelson's Column. He wished he could go in and see their pictures. But only lords and ladies were allowed in there.

The workhouse seemed a grand building too, with a Union Jack flying high outside, and a portrait of the Emperor over the gates. Yet when the guards let Adam in, and told him to hand out the clothes himself, he was surprised by what he saw inside.

There were commoners in the yard – ordinary British adults and children – breaking rocks with hammers. He didn't need his powers to know how miserable they were. They were hunched over, too exhausted to look up, or notice that he was a foreigner.

His heart leaped when he saw Old Jack and Big Jackie among them. But the shepherds were in a shocking state. There was no sign of their sheep, and their rags looked even more ragged than before. Nevertheless, Big Jackie was handing out food, sharing the pitiful scraps they had with the others.

'God bless you, lad!' he said, as Adam gave them his parcels of clothes. 'Here, look, everyone – this nice lad is bringing us some decent clobber!'

Old Jack was still breaking rocks in silence. He hadn't looked up or said a word. His body was bent double, as if something inside him was broken.

'What happened to you?' said Adam. 'Where's Lamb?'

'My Lamb is gone!' cried Old Jack. 'Them thieving lords came and took the whole flock. They is taking everything from us!' He threw his hammer down. He buried his face in Big Jackie's arms, and the other shepherd held him gently as he shook.

'It's over, lad,' said Big Jackie. 'All the land is

gone now. All the animals too.'

Adam wished he had more than a few clothes to give them. He wished there was something else he could do to help them. But what could anyone do?

It was nearly noon by the time he made it to Tottenham Court Road. Again, he heard footsteps behind him, yet could see no one through the mist. No mist could conceal the signs that had gone up around the dump, though:

PRIVATE PROPERTY – NO PUBLIC ACCESS
THIS LAND IS TO BE ENCLOSED

He shuddered as he read the words. So it was happening here as well, just as he'd feared. But what about the tyger? Was she still in there?

'Hey!' called a voice, up ahead. Adam's heart jumped as someone loomed out of the mist, dressed in a cloak and hood. But it was Zadie, waiting for him by the gates.

'Hey, Zadie,' he said, feeling a bit calmer now they were together. 'Are you ready?'

He led her through the gates of the dump, through mountains of ash and rubbish, to the little wooden doorway of the ruin. All his worries melted away as they entered, and the air filled with the sweet, high

scent of honeysuckle growing wild. He smiled. It felt like bringing a friend back home to visit; something he had never done before.

The tyger was in the room where the roof had caved in, and a tree had grown up beneath the open sky. She was fast asleep. Adam and Zadie stood there in silence for a while, just looking at her. Zadie pulled back her hood to stare at the impossible animal who lay sleeping in the half-light.

'I . . . I knew she was a tyger,' she whispered, her eyes shining. 'But I had no idea . . .'

Adam bent down to stroke the tyger's fur.

'Tyger?' he said softly. But the tyger did not reply.

'Is she all right?' said Zadie. 'She's bleeding.'

'Tyger!' said Adam, his insides twisting. 'I've brought a friend to see you.'

The tyger's eyes opened. She rose up onto all four paws, ignoring the wound that still hadn't healed. 'Welcome!' she rumbled. 'I welcome you both, O friends!'

Adam hugged her great warm body. The tyger put her paws around him too, pressing up so close, their bodies almost felt like one.

Zadie stared at them in silence. Then she took a small step forwards, and held out a hand towards the tyger.

The tyger let Zadie touch her. She blinked those eyes of liquid gold: long, slow, trusting blinks. Their light seemed fainter than ever. Yet as Zadie stroked her fur, the tyger's eyes glowed more brightly, and she began to make deep sounds of pleasure, like waves rising from the ocean floor.

It was a moment when time seemed to stop. Adam never knew how long it lasted. A second, a minute, an hour. A timeless time that he wished could last forever.

'Are you really an immortal, Tyger?' whispered Zadie.

'I am a being of infinity and eternity,' said the tyger, 'beyond all space and time.'

Zadie looked at the tyger's wounded shoulder. 'But then – why are you in the form of a tyger? A mortal form that can be hurt?' she said.

The tyger's fur shimmered, and her tail curled around the tree. 'If I wish to walk in a world beside you mortals for a while,' she said, 'I must take a mortal form, like this one. And mortal forms are beautiful. I love all the things this form can do – though I have taken different forms before.'

'Just like in the myths!' said Zadie, her eyes wide behind her spectacles.

'Many of your myths contain half-forgotten memories of me, and of my enemy,' said the tyger. 'There was a time when Urizen and I walked the worlds together, side by side. But long ago I did something that infuriated him, and he has been hunting me ever since, seeking to punish me for what I did.'

Adam's head swam at the thought. He wondered what the tyger had done.

'So what's your true form, Tyger?' said Zadie.

'An immortal may take any form,' said the tyger, 'but our true forms are unlimited, beyond all binaries and boundaries. Even in this form, I am limitless and free. But then, so are you. So are all who have sparks from the fires of infinity inside them.' She looked deep into Zadie's eyes. 'And are you a Guardian?' she asked her. 'I see you have opened some of the doors, while others are still closed . . .'

'No,' said Zadie, in a small voice. 'I'm not a Guardian. My father was training to be one. He never finished his training, but he taught me everything he learned. What do you need the Guardians to do?'

'Take me to the gateway, of course, and open it for me,' said the tyger. Her eyes glimmered in the half-light. 'But if you are not a Guardian, and if you cannot find them – could *you* take me there instead?'

'Gateway?' said Zadie. 'What gateway?'

The tyger's stripes rippled like the currents of a river. 'In every world,' she said, 'there are hidden gateways that lead to other worlds, and to infinity. There is a gateway in this city. That is why I came here.'

Zadie shook her head. 'I'm sorry,' she said. 'I don't know anything about that. And I'm sure my father doesn't, either.'

'Wait,' said Adam. 'There's a gateway between worlds in London? Where?!'

'Only the Guardians know the secrets of the gateways,' said the tyger. She looked at Adam, and Zadie, and the space between them. 'Yet two sparks together burn brighter than one alone. Together, perhaps you could find it, if you wished to . . .' Her tail thumped behind her. 'First, I would need to show you things that could shake your mortal beings to the core,' she said. 'Do you wish to try?'

'Of course, Tyger!' Adam and Zadie looked at each other and smiled. For they had said the very same words, at the very same time.

Chapter Nineteen

The tyger stood before Adam and Zadie in the darkness of the ruin. Her eyes began to glow like liquid golden fire.

'Start with the power of perception,' said the tyger. 'Clear your minds of thoughts, and let it rise up inside you.'

Adam cleared his mind, and let the power rise. He saw the tyger shining. He turned to Zadie, and saw the spark inside her burning bright and gold, just like his own.

'Good,' said the tyger. 'Now, for the power of imagination. Let go of yourselves, and follow me up into the sky.'

'What?!' said Adam, as the tyger gazed through

the open roof of the ruin. He looked up and saw the cloud-covered sky, like a roof above the world. But as he watched, the tyger's light rose up out of her –

– a great stream of light, it rose through the gap in the ceiling, out of the building –

– and soared up into the sky.

'Oh my God!' said Zadie. 'Come on – let's try it!' And as Adam watched, she rose up out of her body too, and followed the tyger.

He didn't want to be left behind; he wanted to stay close to the tyger. So he took a deep breath, and summoned the power of imagination. And then he left his body, and went up after them.

He was flying! He rose through the roof of the ruin, and saw their bodies in the building below. He felt dizzy with excitement, for pigeons were flapping all around him as he followed Zadie and the tyger into the sky.

And still they were rising. He could see London's buildings, tiny from this height, from Big Ben to St Pancras to St Paul's. He saw the Thames, like a great thread running through the city, with all its tributaries. And he saw the chimneystacks of factories and power stations, belching clouds of smoke that filled the sky.

As they flew higher and higher, he felt the clouds

unfold around him. He went through them into open sky.

For the first time in his life, he saw a clear blue sky, with the sun and moon shining bright.

Every part of him seemed to smile.

And then he saw a great river of light, flowing freely through the sky.

This river of light was in constant motion as it soared across the heavens. Tide lines rippled through it like liquid golden fire: a beautiful blaze of brightness that lit up all creation.

He couldn't see its beginning or its end. It was rising and falling in great waves that seemed to extend into infinity.

All along this river of light, he could see streams branching out in every direction. On their banks, he could see other worlds, with other suns and moons above them. He saw an endless chain of them: world after world after world, glowing like islands in the sky.

All he wanted now was to dive into that river of light, and explore those other worlds. Beside him, he could see Zadie burning with the same excitement. They tried to rise higher, towards the river, but there seemed to be some kind of barrier blocking their way.

'We have reached the boundaries of your world!' said the tyger. 'We may go no further. Beyond this lies infinity . . .'

And at her words, they began to fall, as if dragged down to earth by gravity. Together, Adam and Zadie and the tyger fell back into the world. As they descended through the clouds, the river of light grew dimmer.

And dimmer.

And disappeared.

It felt like a door slamming shut in Adam's face. He came crashing back to the cold, dark, ruined building. Back to his own body again.

He sank to his knees. So did Zadie. And the tyger was a bleeding, wounded animal once more; no longer a being of pure light, shining in all her power and her glory.

Adam felt faint at the thought of how close they'd

come to leaving the world behind. Yet even now, part of him was still yearning to dive into that river of light.

But the beautiful blaze of brightness had been extinguished. All those infinite worlds were gone. He could see nothing above him but the iron-grey sky that hung heavy over London, as always. After what he'd just seen, it looked very strange, and very wrong.

Zadie was shaking as hard as he was. 'What happened to that river of light?' she groaned. 'It was so beautiful, Tyger – where's it gone?'

'It cannot flow through this world, because the gateways of this world are closed,' said the tyger. 'They have been closed for quite some time. But the river of light will return to this world when the Guardians open the gateway.'

'Oh!' said Adam. 'But – what if we can't find the Guardians?'

'Cut off from the currents of infinity, this world will surely die,' said the tyger. 'There is still hope. If you cannot find the Guardians, I myself will try to open the gateway. But very soon now, it will be too late.'

Adam and Zadie both shivered. 'Why?' they said together.

The tyger looked up at the cloud-covered sky.

'There is a time, above all times, when the boundaries between worlds are thin,' she said. 'It is the longest night. The night between the end of one year, and the beginning of the next. In this time between times, we will have our best hope of opening the gateway.'

'But – that's Midwinter Night!' said Zadie. 'You mean we only have until tomorrow night?' She pulled her hood on, and prepared to go back out again. 'How do we find it, Tyger?'

The tyger's eyes gleamed. 'Use the power of imagi-nation,' she said. 'Search for traces of the river of light, and the gateway it once flowed through. Look in the oldest places. For in ancient times, the Guardians built great structures to mark the gateways. So seek out the stones on which this city was built!'

Chapter
Twenty

Adam and Zadie left the dump. They walked to the edge of Tottenham Court Road, and let the power of imagination rise.

Adam went out of his body, into the pavement beneath his feet. The concrete fell away, and he saw he was on an old path that had been followed by many feet before, all the way back to ancient times. Around him, buildings flickered and faded.

He felt dizzy. Disorientated. He felt like he was going to be sick again, so he pushed the power down, and returned to himself to see Zadie bent over beside him.

'This is so hard!' she said. 'I could do it with the tyger, but without her . . .' She shook her head. 'Do you ever want to throw up when you use this power, Adam?'

'Oh my God!' He laughed. 'Every time!'

Zadie burst out laughing too. And somehow, it helped. It really did help to laugh together; and as they laughed, Adam felt the spark in his heart glowing brighter. He'd never been able to share his problems with someone else like this before.

'Well, there's no sign of the river of light on Tottenham Court Road,' he said, when they could speak again. 'What's the oldest thing in London?'

'Maybe something by the Thames?' guessed Zadie.

They ran through the streets to the river. Many of the people they passed gave Adam the look he feared, taking in his skin, his hair, his eyes; realizing he was a foreigner. But no one seemed to notice Zadie. Her cloak and hood kept her hidden from their gazes.

By the River Thames, behind ranks of soldiers in red coats, they saw Big Ben and the Palace of Westminster. Adam thought those great stone structures must have stood there forever, ruling over the Empire. They were surely the oldest things in London.

Yet with the power of imagination, he could see they were only a few centuries old. He could glimpse things much older than the Empire, buried beneath the streets; things deeper and more mysterious than the London that he knew. But though it was easier to use the power this time, there was nothing that looked like a gateway between worlds. No trace of the river of light.

'Anything?' said Zadie.

Adam shook his head. He let the power of perception rise as well, determined to use everything he had. But he couldn't even see the pigeons in that cloud-covered sky. Just the mist, which was thickening into freezing fog.

They kept going, searching for signs of the river of light. Instead, they saw posters of the tyger on every wall, and menacing groups of people prowling through the streets.

They picked up their pace, following the streets up past Hyde Park towards Tyburn: the great crossroads where Park Lane met Oxford Street, Edgware Road and Bayswater. Roads to the north, south, east and west all came together there.

As they neared it, Adam thought he glimpsed something flickering in the fog over Tyburn. Was that a hint of golden light he could see, burning warm and bright?

'Hey – what's that?' said Zadie.

'You see it too?' said Adam. This was the first

clue they'd found, so they followed it hopefully, but stopped when they heard the buzz of a crowd. 'Oh, no,' he whispered. 'The Midwinter hangings.'

He'd forgotten all about it. But prisoners were being executed at Tyburn today: runaway soldiers and slaves, robbers and traitors, and people who couldn't afford to pay their debts. Spectators would be coming from all over the land to watch, among them his own family.

And now he could see Tyburn Gallows through the fog: an enormous wooden structure, tall as the trees of Hyde Park. It was shaped like a great arch, with two upright pillars and a long pole across the top. Many ropes dangled down from it. A row of Union Jacks flew beside it, and a band was playing:

'Rule, Britannia! Britannia rules the waves!
Britons never, never, never shall be slaves!'

'Let's get out of here,' said Zadie, tying her hood up tight.

'But what about that light we saw?' said Adam. 'We've got to keep looking.'

And so they pressed on into the crowd. It was vast. So many people had come to watch the hangings. There was even a first class spectator stand for lords and ladies, and those who could afford to pay for seats. It was right at the front, by the gallows.

Adam and Zadie were caught up in the currents of the crowd. They shuddered as they came closer, and saw bodies swinging from the ropes. Around them, excitement was mounting as a prisoner was led onto the gallows, hands tied behind his back.

'Look at this runaway slave!' said the announcer who stood by the gallows. 'He tried to win his freedom by force. Now he pays for his crime with his life.'

Adam's insides turned to liquid. Every part of him felt cold. The prisoner was a dark-skinned boy not much older than him or Zadie.

'I'm not a slave!' this boy was protesting. 'I am free!'

'Then where are the papers to prove it?' said the announcer, as the hangman tied a noose around the boy's neck. 'You should count yourself lucky to be here, in the greatest city on earth, and not whatever godforsaken land you came from. But instead, you have broken the law of the Empire. And now you will hang, in the name of the Emperor!'

The crowd cheered. They started to jeer at the boy, calling him a savage, an animal, a filthy little cockroach.

'I can't watch this!' said Zadie. She managed to find a gap in the crowd, and pushed her way out

through it. But Adam was trapped. He couldn't get out. And as he looked up, helpless, despite his powers – he saw a spark of golden flame in the boy, burning desperately bright. Was *this* the light they'd glimpsed?

The hangman put a hood over the boy's head, and told him to step forwards. The crowd went quiet in anticipation; all the commoners, lords, and ladies alike. At that moment, their sparks were like cold iron in their hearts.

Adam kept hoping the prisoner would be saved by a last-minute pardon. But no pardon came.

Instead, a trapdoor opened beneath the boy's feet. He dropped down into space, hanging by his neck from the rope. The noose snapped tight with a horrible crack – his neck broke under the strain –

– and Adam saw the spark go out as a human being died.

He shut his eyes. He tried to shut all his heightened senses, and push his powers down. Inside him, everything fell silent, though he knew the crowd were all screaming with delight. Every one of them had a spark inside them. How could they watch it be snuffed out in someone else?

He opened his eyes – and as the roar of the crowd rushed back in on him, he saw his own family. They were at the front of the spectator stand, in the very best seats of all. They were sitting with Sir Mortimer Maldehyde, who was leading the crowd as they called for another prisoner to be executed, as if calling for a sacrifice.

And as Adam watched, Maldehyde looked at Adam's family, then at the gallows, and then turned to smile in Adam's direction – as if he knew exactly where he was.

Adam's guts twisted. He had to get out of Tyburn! This was the last place a gateway could be. That golden light they'd glimpsed must have been the boy's spark, flaring in desperation before he died.

The next prisoner was led onto the gallows, and a

gap opened up in the crowd. Adam managed to push his way out. He found Zadie in tears at the bottom of Oxford Street.

They held each other in silence for a long, long time.

Then they walked back through the streets to the bookshop, their heads down, and their hearts very heavy with grief.

Chapter
Twenty-One

It got colder and colder as darkness descended on London. Even in the bookshop, the fire was burning low.

'Scheherazade?' said Solomon, looking up as Adam and Zadie came in. 'What's wrong, *habibti*?'

Zadie shook her head. She still couldn't speak. She didn't even take off her cloak and hood.

'We saw a hanging, sir,' said Adam quietly. 'A boy not much older than us. They said he was an escaped slave, but . . .'

'Ah,' said Solomon. At once, he shut his shop, and went to comfort his daughter. He held her gently until she stopped shaking. 'I promise you,' he said, 'things will not be this way forever. There are people of good will, working for the abolition of slavery –'

'It'll never be abolished,' said Zadie, in a small voice.

'It nearly was, once, in the eighteenth century,' said Solomon. 'It's true that the abolitionist movement was defeated, and very little has changed in the centuries since then – but history could have taken a different course. What if people all over the world had risen up to claim their freedom? We must believe something better is possible.'

Zadie took a deep breath. She went over to the fireplace, and tended to the fire. 'There's only one thing that gives me hope,' she said. 'The tyger.'

'You saw the immortal?' said Solomon. 'Please – tell me everything!'

'Oh, Baba,' said Zadie, as sparks rose up from the fire. Finally, she took off her cloak and hood, and Adam saw the bright blue dress and stockings she kept hidden underneath. 'The tyger is everything we hoped for, and more,' said Zadie, her face shining in the firelight. 'She needs the Guardians to take her to a gateway between worlds, marked by the oldest structure in London. Do you have any idea where that could be?'

Behind his spectacles, Solomon's eyes shone too. 'I heard rumours of gateways, when I was training to be a Guardian,' he said. 'I never knew where they were, but I do know a place where they keep secret knowledge of that sort. If anyone knows where to find a gateway, they will. They may even know the truth about the Guardians!' He polished his spectacles. 'So . . . it's all true? Everything we learned?'

'Everything,' said Zadie. 'The tyger even showed us how to use the power of imagination to see the other worlds!'

Solomon sighed. 'What did they look like?'

'Ummm . . .' said Zadie. She fanned the fire, making it blaze up warm and bright. 'Well, it's hard to describe in words.'

'I could give you some idea, sir,' said Adam, 'if I had something to draw on.'

At once, Zadie gave him a large sheet of paper. It was brand new, crisp and clean; she was generous to let him have it. Adam brought out his pencil and started to draw what they'd seen, building his lines up carefully, determined not to waste an inch.

There was no point trying to draw the whole river of light: it was infinite. He focused on a small section. As he drew one of its tributaries, flowing by the shores of another world, the river seemed to come to life, flowing right before his eyes –

'*Bismillah!*' said Solomon.

'Oh . . . wow,' said Zadie, beside him.

Adam stepped back to look at the picture. It was his best one yet. The lines were as clear as his memory, rippling across the paper like the river of light rippling through the sky. He reached out to touch it, as if he could go through it into another world . . .

But the picture was just a picture. Lines on paper. There was no other world on the other side.

'Have you ever considered training to be an artist?' said Solomon. 'This is better than many of the posters we print. And I know most schools in this land will not accept foreigners, but there are teachers who believe in education for all, and they are opening a new school to train every child who wishes to be an artist or a writer, no matter where their families came from. Your parents should send you there.'

Adam's face felt warm. For a moment, he could almost see his parents sending him to this school, where he'd train to be an artist, like his mother had once been. He would illustrate books, like the ones he'd seen in this shop; he'd make pictures so good, people would pay for them. He would give the money to Mama and Baba, so they wouldn't have to worry about their debts any more . . .

'That can never happen, sir,' he said aloud, trying to snuff out his longing for a life he couldn't have.

150

'People like us can't be artists, or go to school.'

'Is that so?' said Solomon. 'You might think the same of my daughter. But I am hoping to send her to this school. For although she grew up here,' he gestured to the bookshelves, filling every wall, 'not even all these books can satisfy her.'

'There's only one place I want you to send me right now,' said Zadie. 'The place where they'll tell us about the gateway! We only have until tomorrow night to find it. The tyger's bleeding, she's really hurt, and those posters are everywhere. We have to move fast.'

Solomon nodded. 'I have already performed my prayers,' he said, 'so I can take you there myself. It's a long way outside the Ghetto. Not far from London Bridge.'

'You're coming with us?' said Zadie. '*Shukran*, Baba!'

'Is that Arabic?' said Adam, as he folded his picture of the river of light, and tucked it into a pocket.

'Indeed, Master Alhambra,' said Solomon. 'Arabic was the common language of the Muslim world, and one of many spoken in Timbuktu. My enslavers could take my freedom from me, but they could not take my language, history, or faith. I have tried to keep a little of it alive for my daughter.'

Zadie smiled. '*Shukran* means *thank you* in Arabic!' she said.

'And my daughter is thanking me,' said Solomon, 'because I have not left the safety of the Ghetto for a long, long time. But I want to know the truth about the Guardians, and the gateway. And I want to help the tyger!'

He picked out a cane and a coat from a rack by the door.

'Er – Baba?' said Zadie, as she put her cloak back on. 'Won't you wear something with a hood? We don't want to attract attention. You too, Master Alhambra. I've seen the way people look at you. I used to get that look, and a lot worse, before I started wearing these.'

She handed Adam a cloak with a hood, like her own. Adam put it on over his coat. He tied the hood up tight, covering his face and hair, and immediately felt warmer than he had all winter. But Solomon was shaking his head.

'I am a Londoner,' he said with great dignity, running a hand through his silver hair. 'I may not have come to this city of my own free will, but it is my home now, and I will not hide my face on its streets.'

Chapter
Twenty-Two

A fog as thick as pea soup filled the London streets. The night sky was starless, moonless, dead.

The soldier at the checkpoint waved Adam and Zadie through, but gave Solomon a hard time before letting him leave the Ghetto. On the other side of the checkpoint, none of the people they passed even glanced at Adam or Zadie, while Solomon attracted attention, as Zadie had feared. Sickening insults were called out.

'What is wrong with these people?' said Solomon, as they walked through the streets. 'What has happened to humanity?'

'It's getting worse and worse,' said Zadie. 'When they look at you, they don't see who you are, or what

you're doing. They just see that you're different.'

The air was so foul with fog, it was getting hard to breathe. Adam heard other people before he saw them. Then he heard something that made him choke.

'*Out! Out! Foreigners out!*' people were chanting, somewhere away in the fog. Immediately, Zadie led the way off the main road, down a back street.

'Wait, Zadie – where are you going?' Adam gasped.

'Trust me, we'll be safer on the back streets,' she said, leading them further from the chants. 'I don't know what's happening, but I don't like the sound of it!'

'It sounds like a mob is rising,' said Solomon. 'The Empire's wars have only made the rich richer. Now the lords are enclosing the last of the common land, taking it all for themselves. That is why the commoners are so angry—'

'Who cares why?!' said Zadie. 'Listen to them – we have to stay out of their way!'

Adam's heart thumped in his throat. Thanks to Zadie's cloak and hood, he could finally walk unnoticed, as he'd always wished. But Solomon had no protection. And so every streetlight exposed them to attackers. Every shadow held dangers.

Yet Zadie knew what she was doing. Beneath her hood, her head was up, and she was using all her knowledge to get them safely to London Bridge.

As they walked, Solomon pointed out structures that were particularly old. Each time, Adam and Zadie searched for the gateway with the power of imagination. But though they could see the old paths beneath the pavements – and could see now that those paths had run between the trees of a great forest, older than anything in the city – they could find no trace of the river of light.

Solomon grew more excited as they neared London Bridge. It was like a whole world in itself, with shops, stalls and houses built along both sides. 'This could be the place of the gateway!' he said. 'London's history began when the Romans built the first bridge over the Thames, on this very spot.'

Adam and Zadie felt hopeful as they scrambled down the riverbank and beneath the bridge. With the power of imagination, they sank into the London clay, until they could see its history as if it was their own. Time seemed to turn and flow backwards as they watched the river flow out towards the sea.

Adam saw the great ships of Empire sailing south from here, taking slaves from Africa to the American Colonies and the Caribbean, then returning to

Britain with cargoes of cotton, sugar, and still more slaves. He saw all the wealth and power of the Empire in those ships, and all the suffering it was built on, too.

As the tides of history turned back further, he saw Norman ships coming through, bringing conquerors from France. He saw Viking longboats burning the city. Roman galleys exploring these wild uncharted waters. There were no bridges or structures here at that time: only the forest. And all along the water-front, there was no sign of the river of light, or the gateway.

'It's not here,' he said, as he returned to the present, like a diver rising from the deep.

'I couldn't find it either!' said Zadie, sounding as frustrated as he felt. 'Why isn't it here?'

Solomon peered through the pea-soup fog. 'Never mind,' he said. 'We must move quickly now. Follow me!'

As Solomon led the way down Thames Street, Adam heard more chanting. Then the fog parted for a moment, and he saw a great mass of people at the top of the street. They had flaming torches in their hands; blood red sparks burning in their hearts.

'*Foreigners out!*' they shouted as they caught sight of Solomon. One of them hurled a stone, and

Solomon gasped as it smashed into his leg with a shattering sound. Adam shook. He felt certain this was it. The mob was going to kill them.

But then the fog closed in again, concealing them – and in that instant, Zadie helped her father stumble into an alleyway. They made their way down some slippery, slimy steps to the foreshore of the Thames, where a hulking slave ship was moored. Over the pounding of his pulse, Adam heard the mob marching away, and felt a moment of relief.

Yet before him now was something just as dangerous: the rising tide of the Thames. Its frothing waters surged up to the steps, sucked at the gravel by his boots, then roared as they rushed back into the river, taking the gravel with them.

'We can't hide here!' said Zadie, recoiling from the river, and the slave ship.

'No!' said Solomon, through teeth clenched in pain. 'But if we go along this sea wall, we will find the people that we seek.'

Adam could see no people. He saw nothing but danger. Visions of drowning filled his mind, making him gasp for air. The river was like a living thing, reaching up, trying to drag him in. But if Solomon believed coming here could help the tyger – that mattered more than anything.

Solomon was leaning heavily on Zadie as he hobbled on the gravel. Adam followed them down a narrow strand between the river and the sea wall. Then a wave broke against the wall beside him. It was so powerful, it pushed him over, and tore his delivery bag from his shoulders. He let the bag go, and managed to drag himself up before the wave pulled him under, though it left his mouth full of the taste of the Thames.

He staggered on, and found Solomon and Zadie looking at a metal hatch in the wall, far below street level. He helped them haul it open, and was amazed to see a tunnel behind it, big enough for a man to walk through. From the depths of this tunnel, a stream of water was pouring out into the Thames, like another river, hidden beneath the streets.

Solomon went into the tunnel, and up onto a walkway that ran above the stream. 'This must be the River Walbrook – a lost tributary of the Thames,' he said, his voice echoing in the tunnel. 'It was buried as London grew above it. Yet here it is, still flowing. You can bury a river, but you can never stop it.'

He walked into the darkness and disappeared. Adam and Zadie looked at each other for a moment, and then followed him.

Their footsteps echoed around them as they went

through the tunnel – further and further underground, deeper and deeper into darkness – until they reached a stone wall at the end of it. Solomon rapped three times on this wall, then three times more.

A secret door in the wall swung open. Behind it, in a warm pool of light, stood a lady with hair as silver as Solomon's. She wore a necklace with a six-pointed star on it. She stood very straight and still, looking directly back at them, unblinking.

Solomon bowed to her. '*As-salaamu alaikum*,' he said. '*Pax vobiscum. Shalom*, Lady Judith. We seek the help of the Underground Library. My name is Solomon True. You will not remember me. I came here many years ago with my master, when I was a slave. I'm a free man now, with my own papers . . .'

'You need no papers here,' said the lady, her voice as level as her gaze. 'And you do not need that name.'

'Pardon?' said Solomon, surprised.

'I believe your name is *Suleiman Traoré*,' she said, pronouncing his name perfectly. Solomon's spark glowed warmer and brighter. Then he smiled such a happy smile, it took Adam a moment to realize he'd never seen him smile before. 'Welcome back to the Underground Library,' said Lady Judith, as she waved them in through the secret door. 'We have long memories here.'

Chapter Twenty-Three

Lady Judith led them into an underground chamber, warm and dry and brightly lit. Adam's eyes widened as he saw it really was a library, hidden beneath the streets.

Massive bookstacks towered over him, as big as buildings, packed with books and parchment scrolls. On the walls were enormous maps of cities. If Solomon's shop was like a treasure cave, this was like a gold mine: the place the treasure came from.

Adam and Zadie pulled back their hoods so they could stare at the books, and the other people in the library. There seemed to be people from every land here; Britons and foreigners working side by side. Two women came over and tended to Solomon's leg, giving him a comfortable chair to rest on. Others handed out mugs of hot, strong tea.

'So,' said Lady Judith, as Adam warmed his hands on a mug of tea, and breathed in the richly scented steam. 'What knowledge have you come here seeking?'

'Knowledge of the Guardians, my lady,' said Solomon. 'They are a secret order I once belonged to. We are hoping to find members of this order in London.'

Lady Judith shook her head. 'There are none,' she said. 'I know the order of which you speak. They were once present in this city, for Guardians were once present everywhere, amongst people of every kind. However, that order was destroyed long ago. There are no Guardians left in London, or anywhere else, I fear.'

Solomon looked stunned. He fell silent. But Adam couldn't leave it there.

'There's something else,' he said. 'We're also looking for the oldest structure in London. We thought it was at London Bridge, but I don't think it can be.'

'It is not,' said Lady Judith, as Adam sipped his tea. 'It is true that London's recorded history began there, with the Romans, but its origins are older.' She went over to a map of London that filled an entire wall, and ran her hands over it. 'Much of what we now call London was once called *Ossulstone*. It was named after a standing stone known as the Ossulstone, which has stood in this city since ancient times. We believe it is the last remnant of a henge: a prehistoric stone circle, like Avebury or Stonehenge.'

Adam could picture it in his mind. It made perfect sense as the place of a gateway.

'Oh!' said Zadie. 'Could all those henges really mark gateways between worlds?' Her voice echoed around the great spaces of the Underground Library.

Lady Judith raised an eyebrow. 'Why do you ask such questions?' she said. 'Guardians, gateways – what is really going on here?'

Zadie glanced at Adam. He was so used to keeping secrets that even now, it was hard to tell the truth. But with the power of perception, he could see Lady Judith's spark shining silver in her heart, like Solomon's. He sensed nothing there that meant him harm. Only a desire to learn and understand. So he drank down the rest of his tea, and as its warmth spread through his body, he told her the story of the tyger.

She listened silently and seriously. He couldn't tell if she believed him. But when he brought out his drawing of the river of light, holding it high for her to see, she gasped, and called the other people in the library over to see it too.

At the sight of his picture, their sparks burned bright with every colour of flame. And something inside Adam began to feel very still and very small, as if he was standing on the edge of something huge.

'Did you . . . did you truly see other worlds in the sky over London?' said one of them; an old man whose skin and hair were paper-white, but whose eyes were bright and blue.

Adam and Zadie both nodded. 'We did,' they said.

'Then there must be a gateway!' said the old man. 'A gateway, as we hoped!'

'I believe so, Professor Huxley,' said Lady Judith. She turned back to Adam and his companions. 'All of us who work in the Underground Library specialize in secret knowledge and long-forgotten truths. This library has its roots in the lost libraries of Lindisfarne and Granada, Alexandria and Baghdad. And in all those places, the greatest secret was the secret of other worlds, existing in parallel to our own.'

She went over to a bookstack, and brought down a parchment scroll. She unrolled it to reveal a manuscript covered in golden letters, in an alphabet that looked much older than English. As she held it up, the letters seemed to come alive to form a picture uncannily similar to Adam's. A river of light, like liquid golden fire, with streams and tributaries flowing out to other worlds.

'This has happened before, you see,' said Lady Judith. 'The world as we know it is just one of many possible worlds. And all those parallel worlds are connected by energies that flow through a system of gateways.'

Adam couldn't stop staring at the manuscript. 'Who made that picture?' he said.

'My ancestors,' she replied, rolling up the scroll. 'They were Guardians. And they were Jews who lived in Spain, hundreds of years ago, when that land was part of a highly advanced civilization known to Muslims as Al-Andalus, and to Jews as Sepharad.' She pointed up at another map on the wall. 'Their capital, Cordoba, was to its time what London is to ours: the greatest city on earth. Muslims, Christians and Jews all lived together there in peace, working side by side.'

Adam had the strangest feeling as he gazed at the map of Cordoba: as if he'd seen it before: as if he knew it as well as he knew London, though he'd never even heard of Cordoba before. 'What happened to them?'

he asked Lady Judith.

'Their civilization lasted many centuries, even after Cordoba fell,' she replied. 'But it came to an end when the Alhambra Palace was conquered, in 1492.'

'Alhambra?' said Adam. His head felt light, like it was leaving his shoulders. 'That's my family's name!'

'Then perhaps your ancestors were there too,' said Lady Judith. 'Perhaps they saw the river of light in the sky, as my ancestors did, before the gateway shut. For once it did, the violence erupted, the Inquisition began, and most of the Muslims and Jews were expelled from Spain, or executed.'

'That couldn't happen here, could it?' said Zadie, shivering into her cloak.

'It could happen anywhere,' said Professor Huxley. He sat down heavily beside Solomon, his eyes full of dread. 'No one knows how gateways work. But if they are not opened again, and soon, I fear mobs and inquisitions will rule this land as well. Injustices will grow even worse. Neighbour will turn on neighbour. Everything good that we know will be destroyed, as will anyone who is different in any way.'

Adam's mouth was parchment dry. 'So . . . where is the Ossulstone?' he said.

Lady Judith pointed to its place on the map of London. 'It stands,' she said, 'where it has always stood: at the great crossroads of Tyburn.'

Tyburn.

The word felt like a death sentence. For all the warmth of the Underground Library, Adam felt cold with fear as she said it, and he began to shiver again.

Lady Judith was tracing the outlines of roads on the map: roads that ran from north to south, east to west, all meeting at Tyburn. 'Some of the most ancient roads in the land cross there,' she said. 'It is a place where boundaries meet; a place between places. If you seek to cross the boundaries of reality – there could be no better place.'

'We were right there!' said Adam. 'It was hanging day. It was so horrible, we didn't think there could be a gateway.' His voice sounded tiny, even as it echoed around the dizzyingly huge bookstacks. 'But if that's where it is . . .'

'. . . then we have to take the tyger there,' said Zadie. 'And if there are no more Guardians, she'll just have to open the gateway herself.'

'Scheherazade!' said Solomon. 'It is too dangerous to go now, with the mob!' He tried to stand up, to stop her, but he couldn't stand alone, and slumped back into his chair. 'Please, *habibti*,' he begged. 'I couldn't bear it if I lost you too.'

'I know,' said Zadie. 'But we have to do this, for

the tyger – don't we, Adam?'

'For the tyger,' he said. He looked around the library. 'And maybe for even more.'

Solomon took a deep breath. Adam saw his spark flicker, and then burn brighter as his face lit up with pride. 'Of course, you are right,' said Solomon. 'I have done all I can, and I will be safe as long as I stay here, among friends. Now you must use everything I have taught you, and do what I cannot. Go and help the immortal. For her sake, and for the sake of us all!'

Chapter
Twenty-Four

It was morning when Adam and Zadie left the Underground Library. But there was still no light in the sky. It was the last day of the year: the shortest, and the darkest.

They had to hide many times as they ran back through London. The mob was getting bigger as more people joined it. It was growing more violent, too. Adam and Zadie saw crowds of furious people surrounding a bank, pushing past the guards, breaking down the doors. They saw a prison with its gates wide open, and prisoners spilling out onto the streets.

London Bridge itself was under attack. Before Adam's eyes, that great big beautiful bridge, which stood on the spot where a bridge had always stood since Roman times – London Bridge was falling into the Thames.

Lady Judith and Professor Huxley were right. His city was being destroyed. Things he'd thought would last forever were beginning to fall apart.

But in all this chaos, he and Zadie attracted no attention in their cloaks and hoods. They slipped unnoticed through Moor Gate and down to Tottenham Court Road, where Adam's blood froze. For a high fence now surrounded the dump, enclosing it completely. There were official-looking signs on this fence:

PRIVATE PROPERTY – NO PUBLIC ACCESS
THIS LAND HAS BEEN ENCLOSED

There was only one gate in the fence. It was locked and barred and chained. Adam could see no other openings; not a single way through. He stood there for a moment, staring up at it, chewing his pencil in frustration.

'I wish we could fly over this fence, like we did with the tyger,' he said.

Zadie looked up and scratched her head. 'Well, we can't fly,' she said, 'but maybe we can climb? Let's try it, Master Alhambra!'

And so they climbed. They climbed up and over the fence, and leaped down the other side.

'Ha!' said Adam, as they landed. 'But – can you just call me Adam? I've never liked the name Alhambra.'

'Sure,' said Zadie. 'Foreign names are trouble, right? That's why I never call myself Scheherazade. But isn't it a shame? Scheherazade's a queen in *The Arabian Nights* – and it turns out Alhambra is a palace in Spain! I wish we didn't have to hide our names, like we have to hide our faces.'

Adam's skin felt warm. That was it, exactly. It wasn't the name itself he hated, but the danger that it brought. And at this thought, the spark inside him began to glow again: that secret glow in his heart. He and Zadie had so much more in common than he'd known.

'We shouldn't have to hide, should we?' he said. 'Your father was right: we're Londoners too. It's true that our families came from somewhere else, but so did everyone who ever lived here, if you go back far enough. The tyger showed me that.'

'I can't wait to see her again!' said Zadie, as they entered the ruin together.

They found the tyger in the very first room this

time, curled around the tree that grew in there, beneath the broken ceiling. But her eyes were closed. Her body looked thinner. Adam could see her ribs through her fur. Even her stripes seemed to be fading away.

'Tyger?' he said.

The tyger did not reply.

'Is she all right?' whispered Zadie.

'She's fine!' said Adam. 'She – she's going to be fine.' His hands shook as he bent down to stroke the tyger. Her body felt frighteningly still. He wasn't even sure she was breathing. 'Tyger?' he said.

Finally, the tyger's eyes opened. They looked blurry and dark. But she was still alive.

'We think we've found the gateway, Tyger!' said Adam, the words pouring out of him in relief. 'There are no Guardians, but we can take you there. It's not far.'

The tyger blinked. Slowly, focus returned to her eyes. 'Then I myself will try to open it,' she said. 'I will do everything in my power.'

'We'd better wait until nightfall,' said Zadie. 'It's too dangerous in daylight. The mob is on the loose in London, destroying everything. And your enemies have the whole city hunting for you.'

The tyger growled. But she settled down by Adam

and Zadie to wait for the cover of darkness. They leaned in close to her, and warmed themselves on the heat that was streaming from her heart.

'Tyger?' said Adam, after a while. 'Can I ask you something? Why did you choose to be a tyger in a world where tygers are extinct?'

The tyger's tail thumped behind her. 'This stunted little world breaks my heart,' she said. 'So much here has stagnated and died. I wanted to remind you of what has been lost – but also of what is possible. You see, tygers could flourish only when they lived in freedom. And you have never known what it is to be free.'

'What do you mean?' said Zadie. 'We're free British citizens.'

'Imagine how different you would be if the history of your world was different,' said the tyger. 'There are infinite possible histories of the world, and of yourselves. So you should never stop questioning the world, and everything in it; wondering how it could be different.'

Zadie looked up at the ceiling, and the open sky. 'My father always says things would be different if slavery had been abolished, and the Empire had ended,' she said. 'But that's not what happened.'

'The way things are is not the way they have to

be,' said the tyger. Her whiskers probed the air. 'This is a world built on the belief that some people are entitled to conquer and enslave. Until that belief is defeated, no one can be truly free. I fear my enemy has been busy here, hardening hearts, forging manacles for minds, even as he lay in wait for me. It must have been he who closed the gateways, to trap me. I never knew he had such power.'

The temperature seemed to drop. 'But you have power too, don't you, Tyger?' said Zadie. 'If your enemy closed the gateways, you can open them again, can't you?'

'I do not know,' she said. 'Gateways are meant to be open. The Guardians always kept them open.' She looked down. 'I do not know how Urizen closed them,' she said, 'but it is not just killing this world. It is killing *me*.'

Adam huddled into his cloak. He felt cold, so cold, as if he himself was dead.

'But – you're immortal – aren't you, Tyger?' said Zadie.

The tyger's eyes were entirely black now, with no trace of golden fire.

'In the end,' she said, in a scarily calm voice, 'all that lives must die. Even immortals. For we are immortal only in infinity. When we take mortal

forms, we become mortal. And if, instead of returning to infinity, I should die in this world – then I shall die everywhere and always.'

'Stop it, Tyger!' cried Adam. 'You can't die!'

'You must know in your heart I cannot survive here forever, my friend,' she said. Her tail curled around the trunk of the tree. 'Perhaps it is time. I have lived so long already. Witnessed so many worlds and lives. I was there when your ancestors first stood on two feet! Such brave beings, with such potential. They only needed a little help . . .'

Adam clutched on to her paws. 'Don't talk like that!' he said. 'Isn't there anything we can do?'

'Yes,' said the tyger. 'If I cannot open the gateway – then you must. You must become the Guardians yourselves.'

'Us?' said Zadie. 'But . . . how?'

The tyger looked at them, and at the space between them, and her eyes began to gleam again with golden fire. 'Anyone can be a Guardian,' she said. 'Guardians were nothing more than mortals whose hearts and minds were open, and who learned to use the power that is inside you all. So before we leave this place tonight, you must face the third set of doors. Ready or not, you must face the doors of creation!'

Chapter
Twenty-Five

'To open a gateway between worlds,' said the tyger, in the darkness of the ruin, 'you must first of all see the possibility of a gateway. Then you must make that possibility a reality. You must create it. You will find the power you need inside you, if you go through the doors of creation to the other side.'

She stepped away. And there, in the wall behind her, was a new pair of doors, where there had been no doors before.

These doors were enormous. They were built on another scale, reaching right up into the sky.

And they were not made of bronze. They were not made of silver. These doors were made of solid gold.

But once again, there was a crack down the

middle, through which Adam could see a whisker of light. A light so hot, he felt its heat on his face, and feared his eyes would melt.

He reached out to touch the doors of creation. So did Zadie. They pushed as hard as they could, but there was a lock on each door, and the doors would not move at all. They tried using the power of imagination to go through the crack, but that didn't work, either. And all the

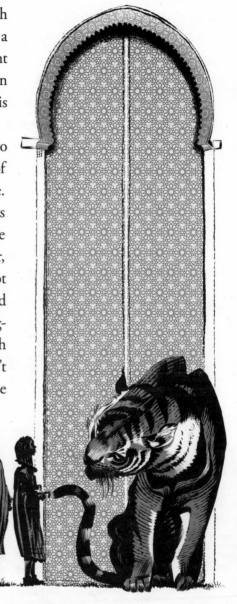

time, it was getting hotter and hotter. Adam feared his whole body would burn up in the light.

'These doors are locked, Tyger!' he cried.

'And if a door is locked,' said the tyger, 'what must you find? These are the doors to your own powers, so the keys must be inside you!'

Adam and Zadie stared at the tyger. And then, in the blazing light of the doors of creation, they looked down at their own hearts. And right there, inside each of them, there seemed to be a key. A key of solid gold.

Adam reached into himself, and pulled it out. He put it into one of the locks, and turned it. Zadie did the same. And with a deep, slow, sighing sound –

– the doors opened up before them, and they went through to the other side.

And now, instead of walls, there were trees all around them. Trees and trees and trees, taller than any trees they'd ever seen, rising right up into the sky on either side of them, and ahead of them, and behind. A great wild forest, extending in every direction for as far as they could see.

'What is this place?' whispered Zadie.

'The same place,' said the tyger. 'But you are becoming aware of its possibilities. For this place was once full of trees, and it shall be again. It could be at this moment – and it is, in many worlds. Now watch carefully.'

She turned to gaze at one of the trees. Adam followed her gaze. He recognized it as the tree he'd seen before. The tree that grew in the abandoned building, beneath the open sky.

This tree had been blasted and bent by the Midwinter cold. Its branches were just bony twigs, with no leaves or fruit at all.

The tyger's paws began to glow with light. The light grew brighter and brighter. And then it rippled out of her, and into the tree.

And in the tyger's light, Adam began to see the potential of that tree: all the possibilities it held

inside it. He saw every variation there could ever be, branching out into infinity.

And seeing those infinite possibilities, he knew there had been fruit on this tree before. There would be fruit again. There could be fruit right now.

Apples. He could see the possibility of apples, shimmering before his eyes.

The tyger reached out. With her claws, she plucked two apples from the tree. She pulled them out of the realms of possibility, and brought them into reality.

'Now taste the fruit of creation,' said the tyger, offering Adam and Zadie the apples.

Zadie took one of them. Adam took the other. He hefted it in his hand; rubbed its shiny skin. He held it up and smelled it. Fresh as springtime. Then he crunched into the apple, and the flavours exploded in his mouth: sharp, sweet, delicious.

'It's real!' said Zadie, through a mouthful of juice. 'How did you do that, Tyger?'

'In infinity, every possibility is a reality,' said the tyger, as they munched the apples. 'There are sparks from the fires of infinity inside you. So you can see possibilities, and turn them into realities. You hold this power in the palms of your hands.'

Adam felt giddy as he reached the apple's core. 'But – we can't create something out of nothing, like

183

you just did!'

'Perhaps not yet,' said the tyger, 'but you have the potential. Every human being has it. At first, only immortals did. But then someone stole a spark from the fires of infinity, and gave it to your kind. So now the power of creation is yours, like perception and imagination. And with these powers, there is nothing you cannot do.'

Adam took a deep breath. He looked down at the palms of his hands, and tried to send a stream of light out of them, like the tyger . . .

. . . but nothing happened. No stream of light. He had only his single spark, burning inside him, alone.

He came away from the tree, defeated, to see Zadie huddling into her hood. She tossed her apple core away.

'I can't even show my face on the streets,' she said, in a wintry voice. 'How can I do any of the things I want to do, let alone something like that?'

'It is the hardest thing of all to see the truth about yourself,' said the tyger. 'I cannot show you how. One day, perhaps, you may find the doors of revelation. Then you will see what you are, and what you can do. But for now – what do you most wish to do? What is your dearest dream, in all the world?'

Adam looked at Zadie, waiting for her reply. He

had no idea what she would say.

Zadie stayed silent.

The tyger turned to Adam, the same question in her eyes.

'I want to be an artist,' he said at once, surprised to hear himself say it aloud.

'That makes sense,' said Zadie. 'And – all right, fine – I want to be a writer! I want to write books about what it's like to be a foreigner in this land; what it's like to be conquered, or enslaved. I think if people knew the truth, they might feel differently. Maybe they'd even abolish slavery, and end the British Empire one day. But what hope is there of that ever happening?'

Adam smiled sadly. He loved Zadie's dream. But like his own dream of becoming an artist – he knew it could never happen. They were impossible dreams.

'Hold on to your dreams,' said the tyger. 'They will help you change the world, or create new worlds, for every time you make a choice, that is what you do. And if you can dream of something – then in all of infinity, there must be at least one world in which that dream is real.'

'Wait!' said Zadie. She threw back her hood, and Adam saw a little sparkle in her eyes again. 'Are you saying there are worlds where no one is a slave? Worlds where everyone lives in peace, and everything is open and free?'

Adam never heard the tyger's answer. Instead, he heard the *clop clop clop* of horses' hooves, and the baying of a pack of hounds.

'Tyger!' he said, as the doors of creation disappeared. They were back in the darkness of the ruin, with just the one tree before them. Its withered fruitless branches seemed to shiver in the cold. 'Your enemy's agents! I can hear them!'

'Yes,' said the tyger, in a voice so calm, it was terrifying. 'If they capture me, they will summon Urizen, and hand me over to him. He will take me back to infinity in chains, to punish me for all of eternity. It will be worse than death, for my suffering will never end. And he will win the war for this world – and for every world.'

Chapter
Twenty-Six

Someone banged on the door of the building. The whole structure shook. Debris crumbled from the ceiling.

Adam was already moving. 'Run!' he told the tyger as he rushed out to defend her. But he froze at the doorway in horror, because his big brother Ramzi was standing there, blocking the way.

'You see, my lord?' Ramzi was saying, as snow came down from the sky. 'I told you I followed him here. And I'm sure you'll find your beast in this building.'

Adam had been betrayed by his own brother. For Ramzi was talking to Sir Mortimer Maldehyde. The lord was right behind him, dressed in his top hat and tailcoat, riding high on his great white horse. He was flanked by the four huntsmen in scarlet, their blood-hounds all barking, their rifles all aimed at the door. With them were four guards in uniform and an iron cage on wheels, big enough to hold a tyger.

'Stand aside now, Adam Alhambra,' said Maldehyde, his voice as smooth as silk. 'We are here to protect the public from a dangerous beast.'

The power of perception rose up in Adam. He could see Ramzi's spark burning like a hot coal inside him. He could see the huntsmen clearly too, and there was still not a spark between them. Yet once again, he could not perceive Sir Mortimer Maldehyde clearly at all. It was as if the fabric of reality had warped around this lord.

Every part of Adam felt cold with fear. He couldn't say a word. But then Zadie came out to stand beside him. And though he could see her own spark flick-ering with fear, her voice rang out as loud and clear as ever.

'There's no beast in there, sir,' she said, as blood-hounds barked around her. For a moment, Adam thought she might fool Maldehyde, as she'd once fooled his huntsman. 'My friend and I were just playing in that ruin. It's empty.'

'What a charming story,' said the lord. He got

down from his horse, and pointed to the fence, and the signs around the dump. 'You were trespassing on my property, you deceitful little foreigners,' he said, his voice growing harder. 'This land is my land. You have broken the law.'

He nodded to his guards. They seized Adam and Zadie. Rough strong hands were suddenly all over them, hauling them away from the building.

'Foreigners trespassing on the land of a lord,' said Maldehyde, his voice now as hard as stone. 'Your families could be expelled from the country for this crime.'

'No, my lord – that's not what I want!' said Ramzi. 'I just want the reward—'

But Maldehyde brushed him aside and leaned through the little wooden doorway.

'Come out!' he called into the darkness inside. 'I have the children. Their fate is in my hands, and so is this place. Come out, before I knock it down.'

There was a moment of silence. No one spoke. The only thing that moved was the snow, spiralling down around them like stars falling from the sky.

Then Maldehyde pushed at the wall. And with a great heaving, groaning, shuddering sigh, the whole building came crashing down, like a cave collapsing in a landslide. It was reduced to a heap of rubble.

In the middle of it was a clearing, where a single apple tree still stood. And beneath it crouched the tyger.

Time seemed to stop as the tyger looked at her enemies, and her enemies looked right back at her.

Then the hounds began to move. They circled the tyger, surrounding her. They growled and snarled and snapped at her.

And then they sprang at her.

They came with jaws wide. Teeth sharp. A whole pack of hounds.

But the tyger threw back her head and roared at them. And faced with the might of a roaring tyger, the pack of hounds turned tail and fled from something bigger, faster, stronger than they could ever be.

Now the huntsmen came for the tyger. Adam's heart lurched as they aimed their rifles at her. She reared up onto her hind legs, until she stood as tall as the men on horseback. She raised her massive, mighty paws. Flicked out claws like swords –

BANG! BANG! BANG!

– and though gunshots rang out, not one of them touched the tyger. The horses were all bucking with fear, and the huntsmen all missed their mark. Yet still the tyger stood there, roaring. And Adam's heart burned with pride for her. He really believed she could do it. She could face her enemies down.

Then Maldehyde himself stepped forward. 'You know you cannot defeat me,' he told the tyger, his voice as smooth as silk, as hard as stone, as cold as ice. 'You know the power I have over these children. Do you wish them harm?'

The tyger stopped roaring. She looked first at Adam and Zadie, and then back at Sir Mortimer Maldehyde. And as she did so, Adam felt as if something was streaming through the air between them.

'Very well,' said the lord at last. He turned to his guards. 'Let the children go free.'

The guards released Adam and Zadie. The tyger dropped down to all fours, and crept towards the cage. She didn't try to fight. She didn't try to run, or hide. She just crept forwards, body low to the ground.

'Yes,' murmured Maldehyde. 'You are mine.'

The tyger did not reply. She hadn't said a word since her hiding place had been destroyed. She seemed to have given up.

'No, Tyger!' cried Adam. 'Run! Save yourself!'

Maldehyde peered at him over his dark spectacles. And just for a moment, Adam caught a glimpse of his eyes for the very first time. They were as cold and empty as the starless night sky. His blood froze at this unearthly sight. Even Zadie was silent.

Just before the tyger stepped into the cage, she turned to look back at them with eyes like golden fire. She was giving herself up so they could be free. Her eyes never left them, even as the cage door slammed shut behind her.

Adam couldn't believe it. This couldn't be happening. It couldn't.

But now the tyger had been captured, the huntsmen and their hounds were returning. They strutted around her, jeering. The tyger didn't rise to it. She just sat there, looking out at Adam and Zadie through the bars of the cage.

'May I have the reward now, my lord?' said Ramzi, tugging at Maldehyde's sleeve. 'I've done what you asked. Now you must forgive my family's debts, as you promised me.'

'You dare make demands of a lord?' said Maldehyde, swatting Ramzi away as if he was a fly. 'Then I will give you what you deserve. When all this is over, you and your whole family will hang at Tyburn for your debts, and the crowd will cheer as you die.'

Ramzi gasped. He began to cry like the frightened boy he really was, and sank to his knees in the snow.

So did Adam. His legs crumpled as he watched, for he knew in his heart it was over.

'Take that beast to my menagerie,' Maldehyde told his huntsmen, as he got back onto his horse. 'I have business to attend to.'

He galloped away through the falling snow. The huntsmen cracked their whips. Adam and Zadie could only watch, helpless, as the cage began to move.

And the hounds were howling their victory song to the heavens as they took the tyger away.

Chapter
Twenty-Seven

The tyger was gone.

Adam was on his knees in the snow. Ramzi was on his knees beside him, his spark as pale as ash, just like Adam's own.

'He – he used me, didn't he?' gasped Ramzi. 'I was trying to do the right thing, but now we're all going to die!' He stood up and stumbled away, still crying.

Adam didn't say a word. He couldn't. He could only stare at the heap of rubble that had been the tyger's shelter. The place where she'd shown him the doors, and helped him find his powers.

Now there would be no more doors. No more powers. And no more tyger.

For the tyger was gone. And everything good in

the world was gone with her.

He sank into the snow. He shut his eyes, and burrowed down into a cold, dark, lonely place, deep inside himself. He wanted to lose himself in there. Wanted nothing to ever reach him, touch him, or hurt him again.

But then a spark of golden flame shimmered into his mind, bringing light into the darkness. And he thought he heard Zadie's voice, calling him. She must have used the power of imagination to enter his mind, as he'd done with his father.

Zadie. Not everything good in the world was gone. She was still there.

His own spark glowed brighter at the thought of her; the secret glow that had been growing in his heart all this time. But if Zadie was inside him – then she would know about it! There would be no more secrets between them.

He felt embarrassed. He pulled back a bit, trying to hide his feelings. But he couldn't hide from the light that was rising up before him. A diamond light that was like all other lights combined. A light so devastatingly powerful and bright, he felt sure it would destroy him.

And now he saw where it was coming from. There seemed to be another pair of doors up ahead of him:

a fourth pair of doors he had never seen before. Diamond doors of inconceivable size, far bigger than all the rest. The crack between them was like a chasm between worlds.

And through that crack, the diamond light was streaming. It was annihilating. Obliterating.

In terror, he fled from it again, and he could feel Zadie fleeing, too –

– and they crashed back to the reality of the rubbish dump. Back to the bin bags and crushed tin cans, the shattered glass and torn-up posters. They lay there, shivering and shaking in the snow.

'Thank you, Zadie,' he managed to say. But he couldn't help wondering what she'd seen inside him. What did she think? What did she know?

'Did you see those diamond doors?' she was saying, as the snow whipped down between them, separating them once more. 'And that light? What was it?'

Adam shook his head. 'I don't know,' he said. 'I saw the same light when I used the power of imagination on my father. But I've never seen those doors before.'

'I've never done that with another person before!' said Zadie. She lay there in silence for a moment. Then she stood up, shaking. 'I don't think we should do it again.'

'No, never again!' said Adam. He looked down into the rubble of the ruin. 'But Zadie – what are we going to do, without the tyger? It's over. Maldehyde's won.'

She shuddered. 'I'll never forget those empty eyes,' she said. 'He really isn't human, is he?'

'Zadie?' said Adam. He chewed on his pencil. 'Do you think . . . is it possible . . . Maldehyde might actually *be* Urizen, in a mortal form?'

'I was thinking the same thing!' said Zadie. 'I thought it was weird that I couldn't see him clearly with the power of perception.' She started to rummage around in the rubble, and found the apple core she'd tossed away. 'But if he's Urizen – why didn't he just take the tyger back to infinity? No, just because he isn't human, that doesn't mean he's immortal, does it? The huntsmen aren't human either.'

'So he must have gone to *summon* Urizen,' said Adam, 'like the tyger told us.'

Zadie nodded. She put the apple core in her pocket. And then her eyes widened.

'Wait a minute,' she said. 'If that's right, it means Maldehyde's only won a battle here. The war isn't over yet. Until he gives the tyger to Urizen – we still have a chance to save her!'

Chapter
Twenty-Eight

The London mob was at its height. The city was beginning to burn.

As Adam and Zadie ran back to the bookshop, they saw buildings in flames. Shattered glass everywhere. Shops being looted; bonfires on the road.

Commoners were even swarming onto the first class lane, threatening lords and ladies. The horses were running wild with fear, stampeding through the streets.

But somehow, Adam and Zadie made it back to the shop. Zadie took the apple core from her pocket, and placed it carefully on the counter. Then she lit the fire.

'All right,' she said. 'The tyger told us we could do

anything with our powers. So how do we break into Maldehyde's Menagerie and rescue her?'

'We'd have to get past the guards,' said Adam. 'And the huntsmen. And whatever else he has inside. And against all that, there's just you and me, Zadie!'

His heart was thumping at the thought of it. So he brought out his pencil and paper, and started to draw, to calm himself. He drew the tyger as they'd last seen her, facing Sir Mortimer Maldehyde.

'That's good,' said Zadie, watching. Then her eyes gleamed behind her spectacles. She snapped her fingers, making a sound like sparks being struck; like a fire flaring into life. 'So we can't break into the menagerie alone,' she said. 'But remember what we saw when we left the Underground Library? The mob was breaking into a bank! What would happen if *they* decided to break into the menagerie?'

'The guards couldn't stop them,' said Adam. 'The huntsmen couldn't stop them, either.' He peered at Zadie as she went to stoke the fire. 'I don't think anything could stop that mob,' he said. 'But why would they do that?'

'Because we're not the only ones Maldehyde has hurt,' she said. 'My father thought the mob was really rising because the lords were taking all the common land for themselves. So what if they found out *he*

200

was responsible?'

'Oh!' Adam's eyes widened as he saw a possibility in his mind. 'What if someone made a poster with a picture of Maldehyde, like his poster of the beast?' he said. 'It could tell them what he's done, and where to find him. It could set the mob on him –'

'– just like he set the city on the tyger!' said Zadie. She went over to the printing machine. 'You do the picture – like that one you've just done, but even bigger and better.' She glanced at his pencil, and waved at the paper and pens Solomon had left on the counter. 'Use whatever you need. I'm going to figure out where to put these posters, but I'll be back soon to do the words, and print it all out!'

And with that, she was gone. It was hard to be alone again, without her. But maybe it would be good to think about something other than how they'd lost the tyger.

He chose a poster-sized piece of paper and one of Solomon's best pens. Very carefully, he made a line. It came out clear and bold; much stronger than anything he'd ever done with a pencil. He focused on it and shut out everything else, concentrating only on his drawing.

He had to get this right. It was their only hope of saving the tyger. So he put everything he had into his picture of Maldehyde.

As he began to draw the lord's top hat and tailcoat, the scent of apples filled his mind. He looked up to see the apple core on the counter, and remembered what the tyger had said about the power of creation. *You can see possibilities, and turn them into realities.*

And as he drew, line after line, he started to see new possibilities for his picture. And the picture began to change. He found himself drawing Maldehyde at enormous size. He was huge: a colossus looming over the world, enclosing it with fences and walls. By his feet, Adam drew animals in cages, and people in chains, suffering and enslaved.

He put all his anger, all his fear, all his pain into this picture. It poured out of him and onto the paper like a river that had been buried underground, and then surfaced in a flood. He couldn't stop it, even if he wanted to.

When it was done, he looked at it, and felt scared of it himself. Yet it filled him with a sense of triumph, too. Because he saw now that drawing had never been a waste of time, or a waste of paper. It was not an impossible dream. This was something he really could do.

The bookshop door swung open. Zadie walked in with a parcel in her hands.

'I stopped at a baker's on my way back and got us some pies,' she said. 'Happy Midwinter!' She opened the parcel to reveal a heap of steaming apple pies.

Adam smiled. Together, they devoured the lot, chomping through the crusts to reach the hot, sweet fruit inside. And as they gobbled up the final crumbs, the spark in his heart began to glow once more, as warm and bright as the fire she had lit.

'So let's see your picture,' said Zadie. She went quiet when he showed her. 'That's even better than Maldehyde's picture of the tyger, because it's true,' she said, after a while. Then she took a deep breath. 'All right. My turn.'

She selected a pen, and began to write official-looking words above the picture. Adam could see the spark inside her blazing with power as the words poured out of her, so big and bold they could be seen from a distance:

PUBLIC NOTICE:
THE LAST COMMON LANDS OF LONDON
HAVE NOW BEEN ENCLOSED!

THESE LANDS BELONG TO ME

And at the bottom, she placed a name and address:

SIR MORTIMER MALDEHYDE
MALDEHYDE'S MENAGERIE,
THE NEW ROAD, LONDON

'That's it!' said Adam. 'It looks just like those posters on the streets!'

Zadie smiled. She went to the printing machine, and began to print the poster they'd created together.

'So where are we going to put these?' said Adam, as their posters came out of the machine.

'The mob is breaking up into smaller groups,' said Zadie, handing him poster after poster. 'But a lot of them are coming into the Ghetto, so we won't have far to go . . .' She tried to smile again, but she was shaking. 'That's what worries me,' she said, shutting the printer down. 'What if they see us while we're putting up the posters?'

Adam gulped. 'Well, whatever we do,' he said, 'we have to do it tonight, or it'll be too late. Do we have a better plan?'

Zadie looked at the stack of posters. Slowly, she shook her head.

'We don't even have a good plan,' she said. 'But . . . at least it's not just you and me any more.'

'Um – it's not?' said Adam, looking around the empty shop.

'Oh, no,' said Zadie, very seriously. She pointed at the posters in his hands. 'It's you and me, and all those words and pictures!'

He gaped at her for a moment.

Then she cracked up laughing. Adam did too; he couldn't help it.

And as they laughed together, they pulled on their hoods, and went back out into the night.

Chapter
Twenty-Nine

It was Midwinter Night: the longest night of the year. Darkness fell on London, along with an icy mist. The mist was red, reflecting the fires that were raging through the city. The sky was the colour of blood.

Adam and Zadie walked through the red mist in their cloaks and hoods, putting up posters as they went. They couldn't see the mob; just its trail of destruction across the Ghetto. Market stalls had been torn down. Temples, mosques and synagogues were in flames. Even the checkpoint was burning, with no sign of any soldiers.

Then they turned onto Broadwick Street, and Adam's blood froze. For he saw his own parents outside their shop, facing a furious crowd, fifteen or twenty strong. At the front of this crowd were the weavers he'd once seen arguing with Ramzi.

'Look at all this foreign stuff!' one of them was screaming, as a bonfire raged in the middle of the road. 'These thieving cockroaches are taking everything from us!'

'*Foreigners out!*' the others were yelling. '*Out! Out! Out!*'

'Don't get too close!' warned Zadie, from under her hood. 'Let's just put up the posters and go!'

She couldn't see this was Adam's own family. But he could hear his parents' voices.

'We only want to make an honest living!' Baba was saying, as Mama tried to reason with the crowd. Ramzi and Hana were holding each other in terror behind the shop window. Adam shared their terror. This was their worst nightmare come to life.

'You is honest, is you?' bellowed a huge voice. A familiar voice. It was Old Jack the shepherd. He was here too, part of this crowd, along with Big Jackie and some of the other commoners Adam had seen at the workhouse. 'These weavers say you is a thief, and we is hating thieves!' yelled Old Jack.

He hurled a rock at the shop window. The window shattered. The words *ALHAMBRA & COMPANY*

were smashed to smithereens. The weavers dragged out a shirt with Mama's embroidery on it, and hurled it into the bonfire. Baba tried to stop them, but with one enormous hand, Old Jack forced Adam's father to his knees, while Big Jackie held a flaming torch up high.

Adam's face flushed as he saw what was happening. These people were about to set fire to his home. They were going to burn it to the ground, destroying everything and everyone inside.

'Adam!' said Zadie. 'We have to get out of here!'

He couldn't. And he couldn't just watch, either. He knew it might ruin their plan if he tried to help his family – but he had to try.

'Old Jack!' he shouted, running towards them and throwing back his hood so they could see his face. 'Big Jackie! Please – *STOP!*'

The shepherds turned and saw him. Their faces were stained with smoke and ashes. In the firelight, their eyes looked as red as their bristling hair and beards.

Big Jackie held the flaming torch out to Adam. 'Help us, lad!' he said. 'Help us teach these thieves a lesson!'

'But that's my family!' said Adam, moving to stand in front of the shop. 'Those clothes you're wearing

– my parents made them for you! I know you're good people. Why are you doing this?'

Big Jackie blinked in surprise. But Old Jack seized the flaming torch from him, and brandished it at the shop.

'Because every thief is going to pay!' he roared, as red mist flared around him. 'Now stand aside!' The rest of the crowd roared too, for they had seen Adam's skin, and hair, and eyes, and the looks on their faces were furious.

Even so, he could not stand aside. He tried to use all his powers, to find anything that might help. He saw the sparks in the hearts of the shepherds. They were blazing like bonfires that could consume him. Yet he also saw the darkness in there, the desolation. That was where the fury came from. They'd lost everything. Now they had nothing left to lose, they were striking out in rage.

Then another voice cut through the night. 'Do you really think *these* people are the thieves?' someone said. 'Are they the ones who enclosed our common lands? Are they the lords of the Empire who took everything we ever loved?'

It was Zadie! Her voice was ringing out loud and clear from beneath her hood, and it stilled the seething crowd. Adam gazed at her, amazed, as she came forwards. But the darkness in Old Jack's heart grew deeper.

'And who is you?' growled the shepherd.

'I'm just a child of London, sir,' said Zadie. 'I could be your own child, couldn't I?' She raised her hands to her hood – and threw it back to reveal her own skin, and hair, and eyes. 'I'm also what you'd call a foreigner,' she said. 'Does that make me a thief as well? Are your hearts so closed, you'd burn a defenceless child who never did a thing to you?'

And instead of running away from Old Jack, she went right up to him, hands open wide in a gesture of trust. At once, Adam stepped up beside her, and held his hands out too.

Then, incredibly, his little sister Hana leaped out through the shattered shop window to join them, her spark burning bravely in her heart. After a moment, Ramzi followed her, so all the children now stood between the shepherds and the shop, their arms open wide. Hana was the smallest, but all of them were tiny beneath Old Jack's enormous form. As they gazed up at him, they must have seemed almost as small as his long-lost Lamb.

Old Jack stared down at them in silence. The whole street fell silent. No one spoke, or moved, or even breathed.

Then a tear trickled down Old Jack's cheek. Then another and another, washing away the smoke and ashes. And now he was weeping for everything he had lost, and beside him, Big Jackie was weeping too.

Adam could see the looks on the faces of the crowd all changing, along with the sparks in their hearts. Their fury was giving way to other feelings; emotions that ran much deeper.

'That's what I thought,' said Zadie, as Adam dared to breathe again. 'You know we're not the enemy. We're part of this city, like you, trying to survive in a world that isn't fair. We shouldn't be fighting each other! We should be united, fighting the people who've *really* taken what belongs to us all. People like that lord,' she said, pointing to the posters they'd just put up.

Adam felt a shudder run through the crowd as they saw his picture of Maldehyde.

'That's the lord who is thieving Lamb!' cried Old Jack. 'He's the one who is taking all the land!'

'He took our workshop too!' said one of the weavers. 'We owed him money, and he took everything we had.'

Adam felt their fury boiling up again. But they weren't interested in him or his family now. They were looking only at the image of Sir Mortimer

Maldehyde.

'*That's* the real enemy!' said Zadie, stoking their rage. She pointed to the bottom of the poster. 'And look – he lives at that menagerie on the New Road!'

'Who is coming?' yelled Big Jackie. 'Who is coming to make him pay?'

With one great roar, the crowd turned away from Alhambra & Company, and began to march towards the menagerie instead. Adam watched them go, hardly daring to believe it. Their plan was working after all. Zadie's words and his pictures had touched something in these people's hearts; opened something in their minds.

'Come on!' said Zadie. 'We have to keep up with them!'

Adam glanced at his parents. Baba was just getting up from the ground. Mama was staring at the posters with a strange expression on her face. Adam wanted to talk to them, to make sure they were all right – but already the currents of the crowd were sweeping him up, into the night, and on to Maldehyde's Menagerie.

Chapter Thirty

Adam and Zadie followed the crowd as it marched on the menagerie. Hope was rising in their hearts, for more and more people were joining them on the way.

'Come with us!' roared Old Jack and Big Jackie, as the two huge shepherds blazed a trail through the red mist. 'Come see the thief who is thieving all your lands!'

The crowd scorched through the streets like wildfire. And with the power of imagination, Adam began to see traces of other fires; even the Great Fire of London itself. Centuries ago, it had started with a single spark, then spread as the sparks ignited: as they merged together and multiplied, making a blaze

of living flame that leaped from building to building through the streets, growing bigger and brighter until it burned the entire city to the ground.

By the time they reached the New Road, the crowd was no longer a crowd. It was once again a mob. The London mob. Hundreds, even thousands strong.

Maldehyde's guards panicked when they saw it. They couldn't stop the mob erupting through the entrances, exploding through the gates. The guards were pushed aside and chased away. Nothing could stand in the way of so many people, all united.

The mob surged into the grounds of the menagerie, and started to smash open the cages. Old Jack

released the elephant from its chain. Big Jackie freed the monkeys and the bear. The shepherds whooped in triumph, and Adam and Zadie whooped with them as they watched the animals run wild.

And now the mob stampeded into the grand white mansion itself. This mansion did not seem so intimidating tonight. It was just a building, like any other. The elephant demolished the tall stone columns, and the mob crashed through the double doors.

Inside the mansion, they found the other cages Adam had once glimpsed in there. They contained two of every kind of creature, from the most ordinary sheep and goats to the rarest, most exotic birds. Even animals he thought were extinct.

The mob set all these animals free. And as Adam watched parrots and pelicans flapping out of their cages and into the night, his heart seemed to soar up with them. For he also saw four horsemen fleeing, their hounds yelping as they scattered in all directions.

The mob moved on into the mansion. But now Adam and Zadie found something so sickening, it stopped them cold. In the biggest cage of all, there were human beings in chains. Slaves with manacles on their wrists and lash marks on their backs, treated even worse than animals. They were huddling in the corner, shuddering with fear.

Then Maldehyde's own slaves came running down the hall towards them: slaves dressed in the uniforms of butlers and maids. They were carrying bundles of

clothes, baskets of food, bottles of water.

'The lord is not here!' they were saying, as they opened the cage and helped the captives break their bonds. 'So come with us to freedom!

They led the captives out of the cage and into the night, seizing their own chance to escape. Adam and Zadie watched them go, the hope rising higher and higher inside them.

But their heads dropped low as they went on into the mansion. For their eyes were dazzled by the crystal chandeliers that hung from the ceiling. Their feet sank deep into fur pelts on the floor. It seemed all the wealth of the world had been hoarded up in here, and the cages just went on and on.

'This place is huge!' said Zadie. 'How are we going to find the tyger?'

Adam tried to clear his mind. He let the power of perception rise. And beneath all the scents of suffering and fear – he began to perceive something else.

Something sweet.

Something high.

Something wild.

'Do you smell that?' he said, feeling light-headed. 'That lovely honeysuckle scent? That's the tyger's scent! All we have to do is follow it!'

They followed the scent through the corridors. It grew stronger as they came to the top of a staircase that spiralled down out of sight.

They ran down these spiral stairs, down another flight, into a basement. And here, finally, buried beneath the menagerie, they found a cold, dark dungeon. There were whips and chains on the walls; racks of spears and arrows.

In the middle of this dungeon was a cage.

And inside it was the tyger.

She lay motionless. Her eyes were closed. Her paws were curled beneath her.

Adam's heart lurched. Frantically, he and Zadie turned the iron wheel that opened the cage door. He reached through with shaking hands, touched the tyger's fur –

– and her eyes opened. 'My friends?' she whispered, rising up onto her paws and padding out of the cage.

'We're here, Tyger!' cried Adam, heart beating like the wings of a bird. 'We did it! We made it! You're free!'

Chapter
Thirty-One

'We must move swiftly now,' said the tyger, in the dungeon beneath Maldehyde's Menagerie. 'Climb onto my back, both of you, and take me to the gateway.'

Adam and Zadie climbed onto the tyger's back. Adam wrapped his legs around her and gripped her shaggy fur. So did Zadie. And they held on tight as the tyger broke free.

They felt her power surge beneath them. She moved as if they weighed nothing at all. She bounded out of the dungeon, up the stairs, through the corridors of the menagerie.

The mob was setting fire to the place. Animals were on the loose everywhere, but the shepherds were

taking charge. Adam saw a tiny little lamb being held up in the air by Old Jack, as Big Jackie herded the rest of the animals to safety. And he could hear Lamb's triumphant bleating '*BAAAAAA!*' as they were reunited.

'Now let's take back the common land!' Old Jack whooped as they left the mansion. 'It belongs to everyone, so everyone can come!'

Adam could see the escaping slaves joining up with the shepherds and some of the others. They were all heading north together in one great wave.

But guided by Adam and Zadie, the tyger was loping away in the other direction, through the smoke and flames, into the night. She roared as she ran down the snowy street, faster and faster, at incredible speed.

The air was freezing, but the tyger's heat warmed Adam and Zadie. They roared too as the streets blurred by.

Behind them, the London skyline was silhouetted against a burning red horizon. But the tyger moved faster than the fire. She carried them all the way down the New Road until it came to an end by the River Tyburn, another tributary of the Thames.

This was a wild place on the edge of the city. There were no bridges across this river. Just the long reeds on the riverbank, swaying as the water rushed by.

'Be careful, Tyger!' said Zadie, recoiling from the river, as she had from the Thames.

But already, the tyger was tensing her body, tighter and tighter, and then –

SPLASH!

– she dived right into the river. Icy water hit Adam and Zadie. But the tyger was swimming strongly, crossing the currents with ease.

'Tygers love water!' she roared. 'Never fear, my

friends – just hold on to me!' They clung on
as she flowed through the river until she reached the
other side. Then she dug her paws into the riverbank
and leaped up onto land.

And now they raced on again, following the streets south, all the way down to the crossroads at Tyburn.

There was no execution happening tonight. No hangman at the gallows. No band playing *Rule, Britannia!* or spectators in the stand, for no one came to this place at night. The Union Jacks hung lifeless and limp from their poles.

But now that Tyburn was empty, Adam could see an enormous slab of stone, standing on its own at the top of Hyde Park. It was more than twice his size. In the darkness, it looked like a door into the night. And he felt sure in his bones this was it.

'That must be the Ossulstone!' Zadie was telling the tyger. 'We think it was part of an ancient henge, built to mark a gateway between worlds.'

'Are you certain?' said the tyger.

Adam leaped down from the tyger's back. He approached the Ossulstone, and let the power of perception rise. This stone was older than any structure he had seen. Its surface was scarred, cracked, weather-beaten and battered. Somehow, it was still standing, rising from the earth as if growing out of it. But what secrets did it hide?

With the power of imagination, he went out of his body, into the stone. Time seemed to turn and flow backwards as he followed it through the ages, seeing everything it had seen, being everything it had been.

He saw that it had stood here through many centuries in which Tyburn had been a place of death. But he was surprised to see this had been a different place in ancient times. For there seemed to be something hidden here that drew people from all over the world.

He saw them coming from Europe, Asia, Africa; walking down paths between the trees of the forest. Paths that had become roads in his own time. Those roads to the north, south, east and west that came together at Tyburn.

He'd caught glimpses of this before. He'd sensed something ancient and mysterious buried beneath the London streets. But now he began to feel he was at the hub of some huge wheel. The centre point where its spokes all met and crossed.

The people were building a great structure to mark this place. They were raising up stones like the Ossulstone, which they'd hauled here from many miles away.

And now Adam felt a surge of excitement, for he could see more stones rising up around him, making the shape of a circle. Lady Judith was right! There *had* once been a stone circle at Tyburn, like Avebury or Stonehenge, but even bigger.

Each stone was as big as the Ossulstone, which was only a piece of this henge. The final piece, surviving on its edges.

In the centre of the circle, the biggest stones of all had made a gigantic arch. It stood exactly where Tyburn Gallows now stood. Adam's heart soared as he saw the sky above it blazing with liquid golden fire.

The river of light had been here! It had streamed through the middle of that stone arch! And now Adam realized *this* was the glow they'd glimpsed last time at Tyburn, before the hanging. It was a trace of the river of light, echoing and echoing through time.

And right here, right now – on this spot, at this moment, and yet parallel to it, somehow – he saw a great arch of marble, shimmering in and out before his eyes. Fountains and flags fluttered beside it. Not just Union Jacks, but all sorts of other flags he'd never seen before. Strange vehicles were driving around this marble arch at dizzying speed, leaving curving trails of red and white light behind them.

Was that another world he could see? Another London? And was that another Adam Alhambra, looking back at him, before the vision flickered and changed again?

World after world seemed to flash before his eyes.

In every world, in every time, there was always something in the shape of an arch here, on this spot, at this crossroads. Even Tyburn Gallows. Because it too was the shape of an archway. A doorway.

A gateway.

'This is it, Tyger!' said Adam, as it all came together his mind. 'The gateway's right here, under the gallows. All you have to do is open it.'

But before the tyger could reply, another voice cut through the night.

'Stop, thieves!' shouted Sir Mortimer Maldehyde.

Adam crashed back to his own body; his own place and time. And instead of a henge of stone, an arch of marble, an ancient forest in the night – all he could see now was Tyburn Gallows.

The place of death again.

Chapter
Thirty-Two

Adam could see Sir Mortimer Maldehyde, right there by Tyburn Gallows. But this time, despite the darkness of the Midwinter Night, he could see the lord very clearly with the power of perception.

Maldehyde threw off his top hat. Long white hair streamed out like clouds on the horizon. He threw off his tailcoat, and two great white wings opened up behind him, like the wings of an angel, or a demon. An immortal, not a human being.

Adam shuddered as he took it in. So it was true. Maldehyde *was* Urizen, in disguise. And that was why they'd never been able to perceive him clearly before. Because his human form was just a disguise.

But now Urizen had cast off that form, he seemed

to fill the sky. His eyes were as cold and empty as the starless night. In his hand was a whip of fire which he brandished like a sword: a great fiery sword that turned in all directions.

Adam felt tiny with terror as Urizen came for him and Zadie by the Ossulstone. He glanced at the tyger, but she was not even looking at her enemy. She was looking at Tyburn Gallows: the place of the gateway.

Her paws began to glow with light. The light grew brighter and brighter. And then it rippled out of her, into the space beneath the gallows . . .

'Escape if you can, my enemy!' called Urizen, fury crackling out of him like lightning. 'But I shall destroy these mortals first.'

The tyger's tail thumped.

She turned from the gateway, eyes ablaze.

And with one giant leap, she soared back through the air to land on all four paws between them, protecting Adam and Zadie with her own body.

'This is between you and I, Urizen,' she growled. 'You swore you would not harm them.'

Urizen shook his head. 'How can you care for such creatures?' he spat. 'How could you steal a spark from the fires of infinity, and give it to their kind?'

'I shall never stop caring for them,' said the tyger softly. 'Their bodies may be small, but their hearts are not, and neither are their minds. I would lay down my life to defend them.'

'So be it!' said Urizen as he strode forwards, wings outstretched, whip of fire flaming in his hand.

Adam's mind was spinning. So it was the tyger herself who'd given the spark to humanity! And that was why Urizen had been hunting her; that was the reason for their war. He wanted to stand with her, and fight by her side, but as Urizen came towards them, all he could do was sink to his knees in fear, and Zadie sank down beside him.

The tyger showed no fear. She reared up to face her enemy, until she stood as tall as him, and her reach was just as wide.

Then she hurled herself at Urizen. She sprang through the air, a streak of black and gold, a blur of living flame. And as she flew at him, she roared at him: a sound like worlds colliding. A sound like the end of time.

Adam felt the impact in his bones as the tyger and Urizen came together beneath the Ossulstone. Their clash shook the earth. The trees of Hyde Park shuddered. So did he and Zadie. Yet they never took their eyes off the tyger. He only wished they could do something to help her. But what could they possibly do?

Urizen raised his whip of fire high above their heads. It came down from the sky like a bolt of lightning. Adam knew it would kill them if it touched them, but –

CRACK!

– the tyger put herself in the way of it. With her paws, she turned Urizen's whip away, taking the blow herself. She gasped as it tore through her. Yet still she stood her ground, defending them.

CRACK!

Urizen lashed out with his whip again, aiming at Adam and Zadie. Again, the tyger protected them. But this time, Urizen hit her so hard, her stripes seemed to split and come apart like threads.

So did Adam's heart. The tyger was hurt. She was off balance. Reeling.

But somehow, she found the strength to come back at her enemy. She hit Urizen once, twice, pounding him with massive paws; pulverizing strikes that could have shattered rock or stone. She hit him with titanic blows, smashing his body, slashing his wings with claws like swords. And now it was Urizen who was hurt, reeling, stumbling into the snow and bleeding –

CRACK!

– but even as he did so, he raised that whip of fire to the heavens one last time, and brought it down with crushing power, thrashing the tyger, tearing her fur to shreds.

The tyger's head dropped. Her limbs and tail went

limp, and like a great stone falling, she sank into the snow by the Ossulstone.

Urizen was badly wounded – but the tyger lay helpless now beneath his colossal form. Adam would never have thought she could look small. Yet at that moment, at the feet of her enemy, she seemed almost like a cub.

'Tyger?' he cried, on his knees. Beside him, Zadie was calling to her too.

But the tyger did not reply. She made no sound at all. She just lay there, frighteningly still beneath the Ossulstone, and silent as the grave.

Her eyes closed.

Adam's heart ached and ached like it might break in two.

And Urizen's great white wings beat the air in victory.

Chapter
Thirty-Three

Urizen turned away from the tyger. He faced Tyburn Gallows, the place of the gateway, and raised his arms up high. His hands began to glow with stark white light.

Adam and Zadie crawled through the snow to the tyger's side. Her fur was horribly torn. There were awful gashes where Urizen had thrashed her chest, her back, her paws. Blood was gushing from these wounds, staining the snow bright scarlet.

Adam and Zadie stroked the tyger's fur. They whispered in her ears.

'Tyger?' said Zadie. 'Can you hear us?'

The tyger's ears twitched feebly. Adam and Zadie kept stroking her, trying to reach her. But her breaths were very short and shallow. And still the blood was pouring from her wounds. With every heartbeat, her life was ebbing away.

'Tyger!' begged Adam, clutching on to her. 'Please – just talk to us!'

Her ears didn't even twitch this time. She made no movement at all.

'What did you do, you thief?' cried Urizen. Adam looked up to see lightning crackling out of Urizen, into the gateway . . .

. . . where it faded away, and died.

Nothing else happened. The gateway didn't open. No river of light came down from the sky.

Urizen tried again. He hurled his lightning into the space beneath the gallows . . .

. . . but once again, it faded away and died. And still the gateway stayed shut.

'I have been trying to open this gateway since you were captured!' said Urizen, turning to face the tyger. 'Why will it not obey me? How did you close it?'

Finally, the tyger's eyes opened. There was still a little golden fire left inside them, and Adam's heart leaped at the sight.

'Aaaah!' sighed the tyger. 'So it was not you or I! The gateways must have closed . . . when the mortals closed their hearts and minds. This is their world, after all . . .'

'How could mortals do what we cannot?' raged Urizen. 'They do not even know they have a spark inside them!' His huge white wings thrashed the air in anger. Adam felt their force on his face as the gallows ropes twisted and turned. 'No world can survive cut off from all others,' said Urizen. 'If this is their doing, they will die with this world – but I will not be trapped here with them!'

He turned back to the gallows and slammed his fists at the gateway, trying to smash it open with sheer brute force.

And though Adam felt each blow in his body, taking his breath away – though he felt the ground shaking, breaking, as the earth quaked beneath him –

– still the gateway stayed shut.

Urizen looked up at the sky in terror. For all his power, it seemed he was trapped in this world by some power beyond his own.

But the tyger was gazing at Adam and Zadie with new hope in her eyes. Did she know something? Something even Urizen didn't know?

Adam reached out desperately for this hope, whatever it was – the thing that would save him, save her, save them all. He leaned in close to hear it. So close, he could feel the tyger's breath in his ears.

'Now,' whispered the tyger. 'Open the gateway
. . . O Guardians!'

Adam felt like he was falling from the sky. There
was no hope here. Only the tyger's trust.

'We haven't got the power!' he said.

'We're not Guardians!' said Zadie, at the same
time.

'The fourth doors,' whispered the tyger, her voice
cracking, her eyes closing. 'Go into each other . . .
through revelation . . . and see yourselves truly, as I
do!'

Chapter
Thirty-Four

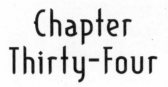

Adam and Zadie looked into each other's eyes.

The tyger had told them to use the power they both feared. The power they never, ever wanted to use again.

She lay silent now beneath the Ossulstone: beaten, broken, bleeding into the snow. Urizen was on his knees by Tyburn Gallows. The world was dying, and neither immortal could open the gateway.

And so, beneath the starless, moonless sky, Adam and Zadie reached out to one another. They took each other's hands, and they held on tight.

And then, with the power of imagination, they went into each other: connecting, joining, sharing everything inside them. Their deepest doubts and fears. Their most secret hopes and dreams. Each one seeing what the other saw, feeling what they felt.

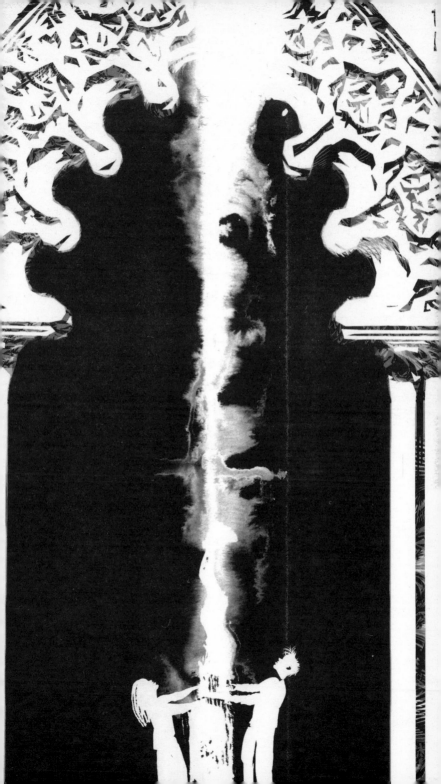

As they did so, they saw the diamond light rising up before them again. The light that was like all other lights combined: so devastatingly powerful and bright, Adam was sure it would destroy him.

It was coming from a pair of doors of inconceivable size. The crack between them was like a chasm between worlds. Adam had seen these doors before. He had fled from them, and from this annihilating light, every time.

But this time, he and Zadie did not flee. They did not pull back from each other, or let go. They trusted in the tyger, and they trusted in each other. Together, they went through the crack between the doors, to the other side –

— and the secret glow in Adam's heart grew brighter at the thought that they were doing this together. Even if they died, at least they were together. But now they were connected — he could see the spark in Zadie's heart growing brighter at the very same thought! She felt the same as he did! And now he knew, and she knew —

— and at last, there were no more secrets. Everything was revealed. They stood before each other without embarrassment or shame.

For they had gone through the doors of revelation. Its diamond light blazed around them. But it did not annihilate them, or obliterate them.

No. It showed them the truth about themselves, illuminating everything that they were, and everything they could do.

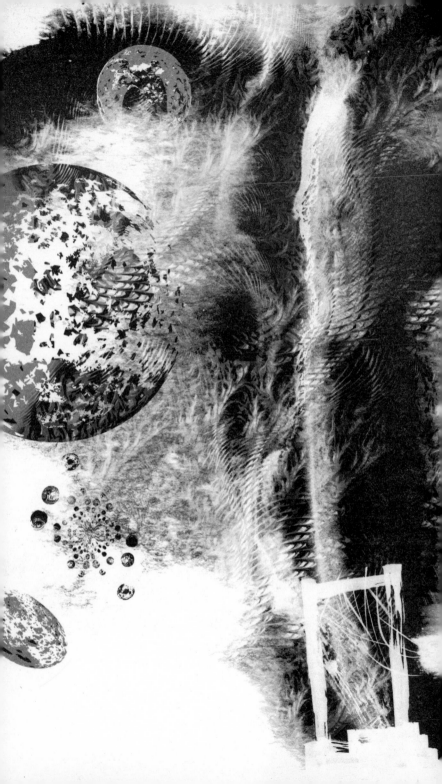

And as Adam and Zadie looked at each other with absolute diamond clarity – each one saw a being of shining light, looking right back.

Each one saw a Guardian.

The tyger was right. They had all the power they needed. They had always had it. But as their two sparks came together, they burned bigger and brighter than they ever had alone.

Together, they looked at Tyburn Gallows. They could see its infinite possibilities. And they knew that a gateway could be open here. It had been before. It would be again. It could be right now.

They looked at the palms of their hands. They were glowing with light. The light grew brighter and brighter. And then it rippled out of them: a stream of golden light that flowed out into the place beneath the gallows, like a river that had been buried underground, and then surfaced in a flood.

As they sent out their light, they felt a wave of energy rising. It felt like their own energy, and yet greater, as if there were more than two of them, somehow. It was doubling and redoubling, like a tide building far out at sea, rising and rolling under the surface, gathering force, gaining speed, then cresting in an enormous tidal wave that comes crashing down on shore, smashing aside everything in its way.

That tidal wave of power grew, and grew, and grew – and then it flooded out of them. As the light erupted out of Adam and Zadie, as it exploded from their open hands and hearts and minds, it felt like a whole ocean of power surging through –

– and like a dam breaking, something finally gave way in that place beneath Tyburn Gallows.

Possibility became reality.

The gateway opened.

And a river of light came pouring through.

It poured down from the sky like a waterfall. It cascaded through the centre of the gateway, beneath the gallows, and then soared up again, rippling away in great waves that seemed to extend into infinity.

Tide lines rippled through it like liquid golden fire: a beautiful blaze of brightness that lit up the London night, as it lit up their hearts and minds.

On the banks of that river of light, all along its endless streams and tributaries, they could see other worlds again. An infinite chain of them: world after world after world, glowing like islands in the sky.

They could even feel the winds of other worlds on their faces. For this was the place of the gateway. And with the tidal wave of energy that was still surging through, they had opened it up at last.

A star began to glimmer in the sky above them. Then another. And another. And as the stars threw down their spears of light, a new moon shone through: a whisker-thin crescent in the sky.

Urizen stared in shock at the moon and stars, the river of light, and all the other worlds, glowing in the depths of that infinite sky. He looked at the two new Guardians, who had just done what he could not. And he looked afraid.

But the tyger was sniffing at the air, breathing in the winds of other worlds. They seemed to be reviving her. Her whiskers twitched. Her tail thumped. And now at last, she opened her eyes.

The tyger rose up from the snow, eyes glowing with golden light. From the tops of her ears to the tip of her tail, every part of her was glowing as bright and as beautiful as the river of light that was shining, and shining, and shining over Tyburn.

Adam and Zadie gazed in wonder at the tyger as she padded to the henge of stone and the arch of marble, through ancient forests that flickered around her in the night.

'You were wrong about the mortals, Urizen,' said the tyger. 'Every one of them can do what these two have done tonight. The power belongs to them, now. Every time they use it, they shall strike a blow against you, and help me to survive. And I shall always stand beside them – in this world, and in every world!'

She roared at Urizen. Adam and Zadie roared with her. Urizen looked at the three of them – the tyger and the two new Guardians who stood beside her, shining with a power that was greater than his own, roaring their defiance – while he stood alone beneath the gallows, wings flapping and flailing and fluttering in fear –

– and that was when Urizen fled. He turned and flew into the open gateway –

– he threw himself into the river of light –

– he fell into its swirling tides –

– and then finally –

– finally –

– Urizen was gone.

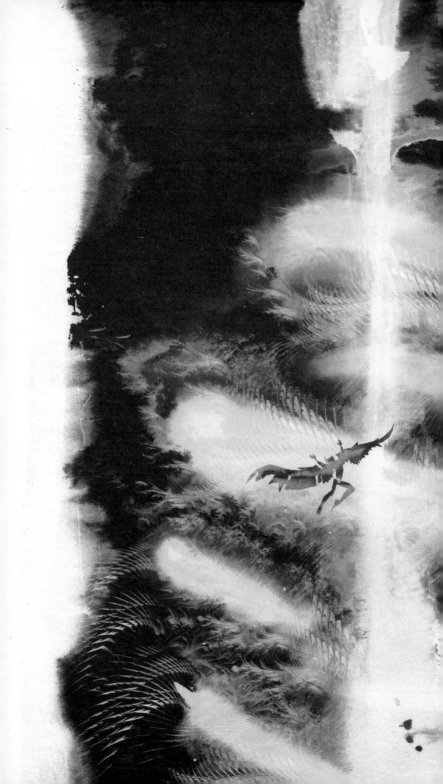

Chapter Thirty-Five

Urizen was gone.

Adam and Zadie stood triumphant by the gateway. The river of light was flowing through it again, connecting the world to all the other worlds and possibilities.

Now the battle was over, they fell away from each other. The tidal wave of power washed out of them. They became two ordinary children once more, standing in the snow by Tyburn Gallows.

But Urizen's whip of fire had left deep wounds upon the tyger. Somehow, she had found the strength to face up to her enemy – but now Urizen had fled, the power drained from her, and she sank into the snow with a sigh.

Blood was gushing from her wounds with new force. And as Adam went to hold her, he saw that these were terrible, fatal, mortal wounds. Not wounds she could survive. The tyger was dying.

She pressed up very close to him. She pressed her beaten broken body as close as she could get, face to face, nose to nose. Adam threw his arms around her, holding her so tight and close, he felt her heart beating by his own.

Zadie joined them. She held the tyger too, and softly stroked her fur. The tyger blinked her eyes – long, slow, trusting blinks – each longer and slower than the last. Her breath sounded like waves sighing as they washed up on the shore.

'O, my friends,' sighed the tyger. 'I am . . . so proud of you . . .'

Adam and Zadie clung on to her paws, never wanting to let go. They hugged her with everything they had inside them, as if they could heal her by giving her their own strength and life and love. But she was hurt beyond all hope of healing.

Adam looked up at the river of light that was flowing through the sky. He couldn't see its beginning or its end. But he knew that was where she had to go. Only in infinity could she survive. Not in his world. Not any more.

'Tyger?' he said. 'The gateway is open. You – you can return to infinity.'

The tyger looked up at the sky. 'Mortals cannot come where I would go,' she said. 'Do you wish me to stay here . . . with you . . . ?'

'Tyger!' said Zadie. 'If you stay here, in that mortal form, you'll die.'

The tyger turned to look at Adam.

He could see all the other worlds reflected in her eyes. He could see himself and Zadie too, tiny and trembling beneath that infinite sky.

He knew what he had to do. However much it hurt him, he had to be strong for the tyger. He couldn't show her what he was feeling, what he really wanted. Because if he did that – she would stay.

'Get up, Tyger!' he said, though the words were like knives in his heart. 'You have to go!'

He pushed her, and Zadie pushed too, until with a deep, slow, shuddering sigh, the tyger stood up. She swayed, unsteady on her paws, but Adam and Zadie went either side of her, and helped her to the gateway. The closer she got, the brighter the river of light burned, and the brighter her own body began to burn.

On the threshold of the gateway, she turned to look at them. She burned so bright now, it hurt

Adam's eyes to see her. But he never looked away. They gazed into each other's eyes for a long, long time. And then the tyger spoke.

'O, how I love you,' she said. 'I love you so much, my friends.' Her fur rippled and shimmered and shone with light. 'Promise you will do all the things you dream of doing. However old you grow . . . never forget your dreams. Never forget the spark. And . . . never forget me.'

Adam's face felt tight. Something stung behind his eyes. But he never looked away, and neither did Zadie.

'We promise,' they managed to say.

The tyger turned back to the gateway. Adam reached out to touch her, just one last time. 'Tyger –' he began.

But the tyger was slipping through his hands. She was moving forwards like a river at its journey's end, pouring out into the sea. And though Adam wished she could stay with him forever – she was leaving him and his world behind. Her fur burned brighter and brighter as she flowed through the open gateway, into the river of light.

The last thing he saw was the tip of her tail, shimmering behind her and then the tyger

      his tyger

Tyger

    was

         gone

Chapter
Thirty-Six

Adam and Zadie stood alone by Tyburn Gallows. The sky over London was no longer on fire. The red mist was lifting. Rain was beginning to fall.

Yet to Adam, it seemed as if the stars were crying. For the tyger had left him and his world behind.

He was the one who'd made her go. But it hurt so much now she was gone. At that moment, he would have given anything to have her back by his side. And when he turned and saw Zadie's face wet with more than rain, he knew she felt it too.

They stood there all night, staring at the place where the tyger had gone. The rain fell and fell and fell on them, soaking them through to their bones.

Eventually, light started to glimmer in the sky.

Adam could hear birds returning to the trees of Hyde Park. Midwinter Night was over, and the world had survived.

But none of it could ease the ache in his heart. For as he stared at the gateway, he could see no sign of the tyger. No sign of the other worlds. Just the familiar London that they knew, with Tyburn Gallows and the Ossulstone at the top of Hyde Park.

'We'll never know where she went, will we?' said Zadie. She dried her spectacles, wiped her face, and pulled her hood back on. 'All we know is that she's gone.'

It was hard to leave that place. In Adam's mind was an image of what he longed to see: the tyger returning through the gateway, roaring, triumphant, alive . . .

But it was just a daydream, and it faded like mist in the morning.

Yet as they turned away from Tyburn Gallows, he noticed something strange. In every spot where the tyger's blood had touched the ground, wildflowers were growing up from beneath the snow, glowing like jewels, shining with impossibly bright colours.

His scalp prickled at the sight. He wondered if wildflowers were still growing in the rubbish dump. And in the ashes of Maldehyde's Menagerie. And in

263

all the places where the tyger had been, and was no more. He wondered if the earth itself missed her as much as he did.

Zadie was tying her hood up tight. 'I'm going back to the Underground Library, to find my father,' she said. 'Are you coming?'

Adam looked away. 'I – I think I'd better go home,' he said.

Up above, the rain was easing off. The sky was growing brighter. And as Adam looked east, towards Tottenham Court Road, he saw something he had never, ever seen before.

The sun was rising. He could just see the top of it, like a whisker of golden fire coming over the horizon.

All around him, the buildings and streets and rivers of London were beginning to shine. The sun was rising higher and higher, growing bigger and wider and brighter all the time. And as it cleared the horizon, and Adam gazed for the first time in his life at that great disc of golden fire, rising up into a clear blue sky, it seemed to look back at him, and smile.

The sun was shining like the eyes of the tyger.

Something inside him lit up as he realised that the sun had always been there, even when he couldn't see it. And it always would be. Even in the darkest night – the sun would still be out there, somewhere in the sky.

And so will the tyger, he thought to himself. She's alive, somewhere in infinity, because we helped her to survive.

He looked back and saw the Ossulstone, still standing there in the sun, as it had stood in the rain and snow, all the way down through the ages. And that was when he made up his mind.

'Wherever the tyger's gone,' he told Zadie, 'I think she might come back one day. And if she does – shouldn't we be here for her?'

For a moment, Zadie stared at him in silence. Then she opened her hood, and pulled out the string that had tied it up tight. She tied that piece of string around the base of the gallows, marking the place where the tyger had gone.

'That's to remind us, so we never forget,' she said. 'It really happened, and it happened here. So whatever else we do – let's come back here every Midwinter Night, and wait for her together until she returns.'

Chapter
Thirty-Seven

It was the day after Midwinter. The first day of a new year. The sun was shining in the clear blue sky over London.

Adam passed many people on the streets as he walked back home. But they weren't a mob any more. Just ordinary people. Some of them were gazing up at the sun and sky in wonder. Others were beginning to repair the damage and rebuild the city.

In the Soho Ghetto, commoners and foreigners were helping each other: all Londoners together, working side by side. In the temples, mosques and synagogues, fires had been put out, and doors were being opened to everyone. Market stalls were being raised up again. It had been a terrible night, but at that moment, Adam knew his city would survive.

Yet inside him all the time was the memory of the tyger. How he wished he could see her again, just one last time.

He got home to find Hana sweeping up the broken glass of the shop window, and Ramzi measuring the shopfront to fit a new one.

'Everything all right?' he asked them, pulling back his hood. Hana rushed out to hug him. But Ramzi just stood there in silence, his head low, his eyes red from crying.

'He's been like that since yesterday,' said Hana. 'He thinks Sir Mortimer Maldehyde's coming to get us. And he thinks it's all his fault!'

In spite of everything, Adam held a hand out to his brother. 'Maldehyde's gone,' he said. 'We don't have to be afraid any more.'

'Oh Adam – please forgive me!' said Ramzi. 'I wish I could go back and do things differently.'

'And what about me, Ramzi?' said Hana. 'Aren't you going to apologize to me too?'

'I'm so sorry!' said Ramzi. 'You were so brave. I'll never call you a baby again, I swear!'

Hana laughed at that. Ramzi began to laugh with her. As they laughed together, the power of perception rose up in Adam, and he saw the sparks shining in their hearts. Yet it only made him think of the tyger, and how alone he felt without her.

The laughter stopped abruptly as their parents came out of the shop. 'What the devil is so funny?' said Baba. 'If Ramzi has really angered Maldehyde—'

'He's gone,' said Adam. 'The mob destroyed his mansion. He had to go far, far away; he won't be back. If we owed him all our debts, then all our debts are gone, too.'

His parents gaped at him. And that was when he noticed Mama holding one of the posters in her hands.

'Did you draw this, Adam?' she said. There was that strange expression on her face again. Whatever it meant, he couldn't deny it.

'Yes, I did,' he said, taking his pencil from behind his ear and gripping it tightly.

'Why didn't you tell us you were doing things like this?' she said, passing the poster to Baba. The expression on her face grew sharper. A terrible punishment was surely coming – but Adam remembered his final promises to the tyger, and knew what he had to say.

'I know you hate it when I draw,' he said. 'And I know the reason why. But I'm sorry, I love drawing, and I'm never going to stop.'

'Adam, please,' said Mama. 'We don't understand

everything that happened last night, but we do know you and your posters saved us from that mob! We would have nothing now if not for you. And this is an excellent picture. I believe you might have it in you to be an artist.'

Adam blinked in surprise. That strange expression: could it be *pride*?

'I think he should be allowed to draw again,' said Ramzi. 'He should have all the paper he wants from now on.'

'Of course!' said Mama. 'Things are going to change.' She turned to Baba, who was studying the poster in silence. 'Aren't they?' she said.

Baba's silence deepened. But as his parents looked at his picture, Adam thought he could see those dying embers in their hearts igniting, coming back to life. 'I swear to God,' said Baba at last, 'I had no idea he could draw as well as this. Has someone been training you, Adam?'

Adam looked down, and shook his head. He couldn't tell them that a tyger had been training him. Or that she was gone.

'Imagine what he could do with training!' said Baba. 'He could create beautiful designs for us . . .'

'Mmm,' murmured Mama. 'Well, even if I'm not allowed to paint any more, I can still pass my knowledge on! But I think he needs a proper teacher. And I've heard that a new school is opening in London, to train children like ours in art and writing. If our debts are really gone, we could use the money to send him there.'

'What do you think, Adam?' said Baba. 'Is that something you would like?'

Every part of Adam shivered with a longing so deep and strong, it took him by surprise. He looked through the shattered shop window at the heaps of parcels waiting to be delivered. 'I would love that,' he said. 'But what about my work?'

'I'll do the deliveries!' said Hana. 'I'm old enough! If you'd just trust me . . .'

Mama ruffled her hair so it stood up wild and free. 'We only wanted to protect you,' she said. 'But after what you did last night – if you want it, the job is yours.'

'Yes!' whooped Hana.

'I'll help too,' said Ramzi. 'We're all going to help you, Adam, any way we can.'

Adam could see the sparks in their hearts reaching out to him. And though he still mourned for the loss of the tyger, he knew the things she'd taught him would always be inside him. 'Thank you,' he told his brother and his sister. 'And . . . *shukran*, Mama and Baba.'

His parents looked surprised. But their sparks were burning bright as sunrise as they began to make their plans.

The very next day, they took him by the hand, and led him out of the Ghetto. There was no soldier in their way at the checkpoint. There wasn't even a checkpoint. Just a heap of ashes where it had been, and some broken bars and railings.

As they walked out onto Oxford Street, Adam's first thought was to put his hood back up. But some of the people they passed gave him a look he'd never seen before. They were smiling at him, as if they weren't seeing his skin, or hair, or eyes; just a boy and his proud parents, on their way to school. And so he smiled back at them. He kept his hood down, his head up, and his face open to the world.

'There's one more thing I'd like,' he told his parents as they walked together. 'I want to know more about our history, our language, our faith. The places our ancestors came from. And most of all, I want to know about the Alhambra Palace in Spain!'

'*Al-Hamra?*' Baba stroked his beard. 'Well, if you're going to start speaking Arabic, you should know our name is really pronounced *Al-Hamra*, not *Alhambra*! I promise, we'll tell you everything we know, very soon. But right now –'

'Hey, Adam!' called a voice up ahead. It was Zadie, waiting at the school gates. Solomon was beside her, leaning on his cane. They were gazing up with pure delight at the sun that was shining down on them, like the eyes of the tyger. And seeing them once again, Adam's smile grew wider. For he knew now that he was not alone. And he never had been.

There was a small crowd waiting with them: young Londoners whose families had come from many places, just like their own. Then some people came out to open the gates. A lady with hair as silver as Solomon's, and an old man with bright blue eyes. And with Lady Judith and Professor Huxley were teachers and librarians from every land, British and foreign side by side, as they had been in the Underground Library.

'Welcome to your new school!' said Professor Huxley. 'It is good to see you all safely here. These are dangerous times for everyone in this land. And yet, for the first time in many years, it also feels as if change might be in the air. So please: come in, come in. We have a great deal of work to do, and we will start right away!'

Many years later, on a starry Midwinter Night, two people met in secret at Tyburn.

One of them was an artist.

The other was a writer.

Many things had happened in their lives.

But Adam and Zadie had never forgotten the tyger.

So even as they did all the things they dreamed of doing – as Adam became an artist, and Zadie became a writer; as she wrote all her books, and he illustrated every one – every Midwinter Night, there they were, back at Tyburn.

And even as the world changed around them – as the gallows came down, replaced by a monument to mark the abolition of slavery; as the Empire ended, and the flags of other lands went up to join the Union

Jacks – there they were, every year, without fail. An artist and a writer, with some hot apple pies to keep them warm through the night.

Together, they waited, and waited, and waited for the tyger.

However old they grew, they never stopped waiting.

They stayed there at the great crossroads, where the Ossulstone stood through winters, springs, summers, autumns, as year after year went by.

All that time, they'd never once caught a glimpse of the tyger.

But on this one night – this starry, moonlit Midwinter Night – the air around them filled with a sweet, high, musky scent, like honeysuckle growing wild.

'Adam?' said Zadie, her eyes shining in the night. 'Remember that smell?'

'Of course!' he said, feeling a thrill he hadn't felt for such a long, long time. 'I'll never forget!'

High over London, the sky opened up –

– and a river of light came pouring through.

It came down from the sky like a waterfall, cascading through the centre of the gateway, then soaring up again in great waves that extended into infinity. On its banks, all along its streams and

tributaries, they could see other worlds, with other suns and moons above them. And they felt the sparks inside them yearning to dive into that river of light, and explore its endless possibilities.

And now, from the centre of the gateway, they heard a voice.

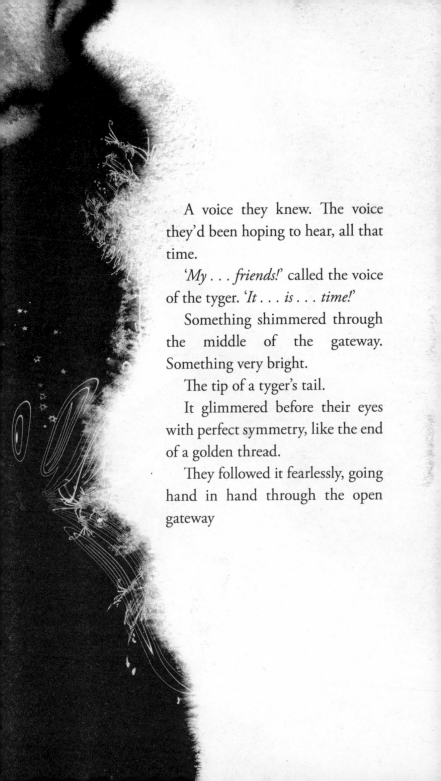

A voice they knew. The voice they'd been hoping to hear, all that time.

'*My . . . friends!*' called the voice of the tyger. '*It . . . is . . . time!*'

Something shimmered through the middle of the gateway. Something very bright.

The tip of a tyger's tail.

It glimmered before their eyes with perfect symmetry, like the end of a golden thread.

They followed it fearlessly, going hand in hand through the open gateway

and like sparks rising, soaring,
streaming up into liquid golden fire,
they flew into the swirling tides,
into the river of light

flying higher and higher and higher

together, side by side

beyond all boundaries

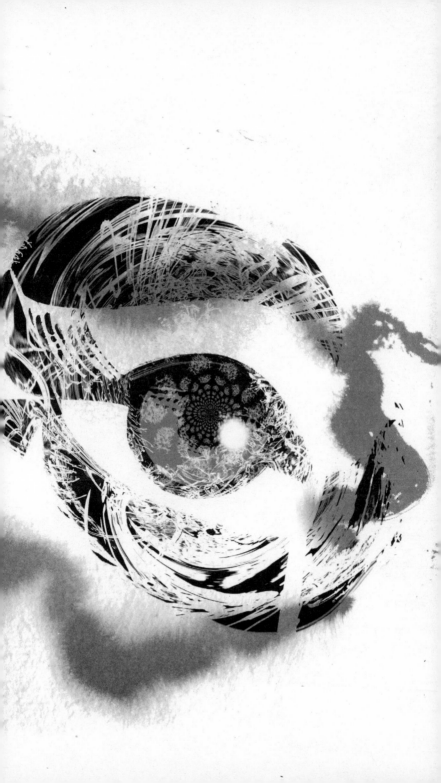

and

into

infinity